TWISTED TALES

2022

ASTONISHING ADVENTURES

Edited By Roseanna Caswell

First published in Great Britain in 2022 by:

Young Writers
Remus House
Coltsfoot Drive
Peterborough
PE2 9BF
Telephone: 01733 890066
Website: www.youngwriters.co.uk

Printed and bound in the UK by BookPrintingUK
Website: www.bookprintinguk.com
YB0MA0011A

FOREWORD

Welcome, Reader!

Are you ready to step into someone else's shoes
and experience a new point of view?

For our latest competition *Twisted Tales,* we challenged
secondary school students to write a story in just
100 words that shows us another side to the story.
They could add a twist to an existing tale, show us
a new perspective or simply write an original tale.
They were given optional story starters and plot
ideas for a spark of inspiration, and encouraged to
consider the impact of narrative voice and theme.

The authors in this anthology have given us some
unique new insights into tales we thought we knew,
and written stories that are sure to surprise! The
result is a thrilling and absorbing collection of stories
written in a variety of styles, and it's a testament
to the creativity of these young authors.

Here at Young Writers it's our aim to inspire the
next generation and instill in them a love of creative
writing, and what better way than to see their work
in print? The imagination and skill within these pages
are proof that we might just be achieving that aim!
Congratulations to each of these fantastic authors.

CONTENTS

Connie Tripp (12) 40
Junaidah Phiri (13) 41
Faith Manu-Cato (12) 42
Galisia Svetlomirova (13) 43
Madinah Hussain (13) 44
Tayla Boulton-Treharne (12) 45
Alesia Rus (12) 46
Mario Toshev (12) 47
Laura Harrison-Algaba (14) 48
Jaydon Broadley (13) 49
Asma Ali (12) 50
Vince Taylor (12) 51
Muhammad Athar (12) 52
Brody Carter-Edwards (12) 53
Danaya Georgieva (13) 54
Aya Nariman (12) 55
Lukas (12) 56
Phoebe Jones (13) 57
Oliver Jobbins (13) 58
Eva-Raquel Jurca Latienda (12) 59
Ibrahim Riaz (13) 60
Solomon Hylton (13) 61
Ryan Sutton-Lucas (12) 62
Danny Bennett (13) 63
Anisah Mulk (13) 64

Bury CE High School, Haslam Brow

Matilda Unsworth (15) 65
Charlotte Plant (13) 66

Cambourne Village College, Cambourne

Amos Leung 67
Harriet Foggo (12) 68

Chichester Free School, Bognor Regis

Isabella Blythe (13) 69

Clifton High School, Clifton

Nate Barnes (13) 70
Louis Watts (13) 71
Harrison Taylor (12) 72
Andrew Carter (13) 73
Sam Motherwell (13) 74
Alfie England (13) 75

Co-Op Academy Bebington, Bebington

Alicia Davies (13) 76
Kieran Scott (14) 77

Coedcae School, Llanelli

Anya Williams (12) 78
Layla Esposito-Williams (13) 79
Rojda Otag (13) 80

Cove School, Cove

Zoë Thomson (13) 81
Sophie Thomson (12) 82

Craigroyston Community High School, Edinburgh

Riley Conyon (13) 83
Judy Akhdier (13) 84

Cyfarthfa High School Lower, Merthyr Tydfil

Hannah May Warr (13) 85
Jayden Simons (13) 86
Ruby Jones (13) 87
Reuben Lackman-Jones (13) 88

Denstone College, Denstone

Jonas Mullington (12) 89
Keatan Bagraith (15) 90
Seth Harrison (13) 91

Forres Academy, Forres

Konrad Wilk (14)	92

Gairloch High School, Gairloch

Maisie Gordon (13)	93

Hazel Grove High School, Hazel Grove

Emelia Maddocks (12)	94
Georgia Brown (13)	95
Emilia Twemlow (12)	96
Jessica Lancaster (12)	97
Maggie Bradburn (13)	98
Faith Hughes (13)	99
Benji Fox (12)	100
Elicia Lewis (14)	101
Raeesa Hossain (12)	102
Merrily Maunder (13)	103
Jacob Newman (12)	104
Jasmine Heslin (12)	105
Max Horley (12)	106
Lacia Keay (11)	107
Grace Stonier (12)	108
Jamie Parlby (13)	109
Ellie McGregor (12)	110
Amy Atkins (12)	111
Oliver Poole (12)	112
Jyles Hazlewood (11)	113
Joey Standard (12)	114
Oliver Kibble (13)	115

Helston Community College, Helston

Selena Payne (12)	116
Matilda Stringer (13)	117

Holy Trinity Catholic School, Small Heath

Aisha Fazeel (12)	118

John Cabot Academy, Kingswood

Evelyn Houlden (13)	119

King Alfred's Academy, Wantage

Ella Morgan Bailey (14)	120

King Edward VI High School For Girls, Birmingham

Nayana Pillay (15)	121

Kingsland School, Watersheddings

Lily Stevenson (14)	122

Langley Park School For Girls, Beckenham

Dhaani Pandya (11)	123
Laura Sullivan (14)	124
Isabella Travers (14)	125
Amélie Holst (14)	126
Anna Greenwood (14)	127
Mia Forrest (14)	128
Daisy Wallace (14)	129
Yasmine Amrane (14)	130
Megan Ofori-Appiah (12)	131
Emma Wallace (14)	132
Zahra Haman (11)	133
Kitty-Mae Brown (14)	134
Emma Wilson (14)	135
Isla Wilton (12)	136
Demi-Mae Woolcott (14)	137
Chesney Paul (14)	138
Sahar Attaran (14)	139
Alicia Boscornea (14)	140
Evie Kench (14)	141

Southend High School For Boys, Westcliff-On-Sea

Aidan Clarke (12)	177

Southfields Academy, Wandsworth

Gjulio Gjoka	178

St Andrew's CE High School, Worthing

Kai Howell (12)	179

St Augustine Academy, Maidstone

Jade Fleet (15)	180

St Barnabas CE First & Middle School, Drakes Broughton

Sophie Cosnett (12)	181
Ashton Cox (12)	182
Barnaby Boucker (12)	183

St Catherine's School, Bramley

Annie Fichardt (12)	184
Charlotte Ebsworth (13)	185

Sybil Andrews Academy, Bury St Edmunds

Samuel Clare (12)	186
Lucas Palframan (12)	187
Joshua Campbell-Hissett (11)	188
Coby Alton (12)	189
Travis Hope (11)	190

Tarporley High School, Tarporley

Daisy Sturdey (12)	191

Teenage Kicks, Failsworth

Adam Butt (13)	192
Fiona Collins (15)	193
Skye Robinson (15)	194

The Community College, Bishops Castle

Samuel Burke (13)	195

The Open Academy, Norwich

Isla Gardner (15)	196
James Hoye (15)	197
Lisa Kracewicz (15)	198

The Roseland Academy, Tregony

Daniel Mawby (13)	199

The Royal Liberty School, Gidea Park

Matas Konstantinov (14)	200
Revin Kazim (13)	201
Aqeel Miah (14)	202
Ashleigh Wansi (14)	203
Bipin Acharya (13)	204
Varun Teeluck (14)	205
Liam Kelly (14)	206
Azuolas Kersevicius (13)	207
Oliver Roberts (14)	208
Aleksas Martinkus (14)	209
Christian Stanley (13)	210
Teddy Wells (13)	211
Lee Fisher (13)	212
Tommy Randall (13)	213

The Ursuline Academy Ilford, Ilford

Amelia Ali (12)	214

Trinity Academy, Leeds

Najma Mohamed (12)   215

Turning Point Academy, Ormskirk

Alex Robertson (15)   216
Keiran Mullock (15)   217

Tuxford Academy, Tuxford

Louie Burman (13)   218
Auguste Birbalaite (14)   219

Twickenham School, Whitton

Maryam Mirza (12)   220

Ursuline High School, Wimbledon

Charlotte Porter (13)   221
Gaia Lai (12)   222
Ines Cruz (12)   223
Sophia Brique (13)   224
Eva Fletcher (13)   225
Hiba Usama (13)   226
Keira Nair (13)   227

Waterhead Academy, Oldham

George Mills (13)   228
Lola Williams (12)   229
Anees Hussain (13)   230
Alfie Riley (12)   231

Wellfield Community School, Wingate

Alfie Ryan (12)   232
Aioan Hall (12)   233

West Derby School, West Derby

Ellis Yates (13)   234

Westfield Academy, Yeovil

Esha Ajith (14)   235

Winterbourne Academy, Winterbourne

Kiara Huntly (12)   236

Workington Academy, Workington

Bethany Burns   237

THE
STORIES

THREE LITTLE PIGS: THE HUGE TWIST!

Narrator: I found a portal that led to a familiar world. I jumped in and quickly realised it was the world of the three little pigs. I was at the point where the Big Bad Wolf was about to blow the brick house!

Big Bad Wolf: "I'll huff and I will puff and I will blow your house down!"

Narrator: The Big Bad Wolf blew hard enough for the house to blow down, the pigs were then horrified!

Pig One: "Somebody! Help!"

Narrator: I started running towards the pigs and grabbed them. I managed to take them to their mothers.

Samuel Rees (12)
Aberdare Community School, Aberdare

THE MONSTER

There was a boy playing with a paper boat on a cold, rainy night. The boy's boat fell down a drain where there was a mysterious monster. The boy's brother saw a scene. The boy's brother started to make a plan to kill it. The gang found the monster's hideout and tried to kill it. After some fighting, the monster suddenly cried in pain but nobody knew why. Suddenly it appeared, the pyramid head. Someone read about him and knew to kill the monster. The monster got restrained by a lot of rusty metal beams and got crushed to death.

TJ May
Aberdare Community School, Aberdare

PETER PAN

Once, there was a boy called Peter Pan. Peter Pan was the little boy who never grew up but he was a strong fighter. He could fly. But then everything changed, he was about to face another fighter. His name was Captain Hook. He was fighting him until when Peter Pan turned around for a second and turned back. He got stabbed in the belly then a miracle happened. Somehow he came back to life and killed Captain Hook. Everyone celebrated him in his victory but then everyone gave him a cake. When he ate them he died. Everyone laughed.

Callum Rodda (12)
Aberdare Community School, Aberdare

GOLDILOCKS

Once upon a time, there was a girl, Goldilocks. She was walking into the woods to get some apples for her family, little did they know that wasn't her plan... A few days ago she saw a hut in the woods, she wanted to go back and give it a look. She walked into the house and saw some really cool stuff and decided to put them in her bag. Suddenly she heard the door open and hid as quick as she could. The only place she could seem to find was under the bed. That was a mistake...

Teyah Rooke (12)
Aberdare Community School, Aberdare

GOLDILOCKS AND HER MEAN END

The plan was in motion. The porridge was set and all that was left was the waiting game. The rain punched at the window and stomped on the roof. The forest wildlife fell silent as Little Miss Goldilocks fought against the strong winds; striving to find shelter. There it was, finally a warm place to rest. Goldilocks thudded on the door, but no answer. Curiously, she walked around to the window left ajar. The forest watched. Goldilocks opened the gap and climbed in. The bear's jaws clamped down on Goldilocks' plaits, throwing her around violently until... she just lay there.

Matt Kostuch (16)
Alderbrook School, Solihull

THE ENTITY

The air smells strongly of salt. Its potent breath disseminates to its surroundings, like gossip of murder. The very nature of this thing is evil, pure evil. Its Stygian silver shadows the cerulean sky; casting away any light from coming through. The entity grows bigger every second, consuming everything in its path. Trees are no longer trees but roots left anchoring onto the Earth. Cars are continuously being catered off into its mouth. It's getting closer. But before I can reach the door, my fingers go numb. I break out into a cold sweat. Paralysed. It has got me...

Anuj Mistry (15)
Alderbrook School, Solihull

THE LAUGHTER

Why are they laughing? I want them to stop. Make them stop, now! The voices don't stop. I'm causing no harm, I'm trying to fix humanity and they stand there laughing. I'm not going crazy but I see and hear more. I feel powerful, godly. Suddenly, I enjoy the laughter. So much so, that I myself am bursting with laughter. What makes me laugh like this, I don't know. I see their smiles, their teeth glistening. I want their smiles. I am going to take them. The thought of ripping their smiles off makes me laugh. Soon, they won't laugh.

Kevin Burns (15)

Alderbrook School, Solihull

THE NOBODY

Nobody knows me, except Sharron from book club. I am Dave, just Dave. I have no last name. I don't tell anyone, it's too hard to explain. But back to me, I am sat in my lair. Well, abandoned fifth-floor flat. I am just a Dave sat in food-stained jogging bottoms. The window smashes open and Beetle-Man crawls through. Beetle-Man is a part of the M.P.C. (Must Protect Civilians).
"Man, I just got that cleaned! You owe me!" I shout.
Beetle-Man replies, "No, you owe me." He shows me a bill for ten million dollars...

Lara Kidd (12)
Alderbrook School, Solihull

THE VILLAIN'S VIEW

Everyone thinks they know her story. For aeons, she had been depicted as a ghoulish monster, a monster that would stop at nothing to harm a sweet, innocent child. But they were wrong. For her story started years before the little one's birth, in the forbidden, yet enchanted forest. She had met a young boy and had fallen into a deep but unfortunate love. Her naivety led her to the betrayal by the very boy she loved. He had taken something; something that belonged to her. This was what led to her hatred. This was what led to her revenge.

Gurpreet Bansal (17)
Alderbrook School, Solihull

WE ARE VENOM

The bullets penetrated effortlessly. I finished the battle off like eating a piece of cake. But I suddenly found myself being bellowed at by a lady. She was laughing at me and saying, "You're such a freak."
I replied, "Okay? I don't need to know."
She showed me a video of me acting weird in a restaurant. It was from a CCTV camera. She explained how I was jumping into the lobster tank and eating all of the food. It wasn't my fault. I had a living parasite inside me. No one knew the truth about me.

Max Hawker (12)
Alderbrook School, Solihull

OUT OF THE ORDINARY

Ever since I was a young boy, people have described me as twisted. I don't deny this remark. However, I would have preferred diabolical. You see, I wasn't always this devious, scheming mastermind, I was your average child; brown hair, average height, just a plain old basic boy with abusive, neglectful parents. I tried to make the best of it, but as soon as other kids knew, *bang!* My whole world changed. Kids were cruel, even worse than my parents. It came to the point where I knew something had to change, I had to change.

William Stocks (15)
Alderbrook School, Solihull

RECOLLECTION

I stood still like a statue upon the mountaintops; *how did I end up this way?* This facade, it wasn't me. Though I then towered above those who wronged me, above everything, I had wronged myself. I once stared longingly at the family homes, blood drenched across these dear hands. Tens... hundreds... thousands... I would not shy away from my past, but I could not allow this to become my present!
This mask of agony vanished before my eyes - I could not slaughter who I was, who I am... However, this was my recollection.

Oliver Haynes (15)
Alderbrook School, Solihull

VOLDEMORT'S VIEW

My life wasn't fair. Stuck in an orphanage from the day I was born, finding out that my father was a cruel, spiteful man who left my mum when he learned her true identity. Well, as soon as I figured that out, I wasn't going to keep his hideous name, Tom Riddle. I fashioned myself a new name, a name that one day everyone would fear. Voldemort. And as my dad was a horrible Muggle, from now on, all Muggles and Mudbloods would perish so that I could rule a pure-blood society. Well, at least after I'd vanquished Harry Potter.

Hannah Crowford (13)
Alderbrook School, Solihull

THE TERRIFYING TEACHER

My dreams had come true, I'd finally become a teacher; it was the best day. That was until I realised what a nightmare it was. The more time went on, the more I despised the job and my class. I came up with a plan to make my life easier. Day by day, one by one - I'd make the children disappear, never to be seen again. Surprisingly, I was never considered a subject. I would report them missing after break and act like the upset, caring teacher. How many kids did I make disappear? That's a number I'll never share.

Phoebe Hill (15)
Alderbrook School, Solihull

TRUTHS AND WHYS

We've all heard of Jack and Jill who went up the hill, yet we were never told the reason why Jack fell down. They're both promoted as sweet, innocent children but at the end of the day, we were never told the truth. Maybe he was clumsy? Or the weather was bad? Unfortunately, no. Jack was pushed, by his own sister and in coherence with her plan, he plummeted to his demise. Why? Well, she was jealous of him and the attention he gained from his looks. Although, if she killed Jack, why did Jill come tumbling after?

Harriet Farrar-Hockley (14)
Alderbrook School, Solihull

I AM VECNA AND I ALWAYS WILL BE

It's a big day. I have finally decided to take over Hawkins because that's what I do best and to do that, I'll need to kill everyone. I need to hunt people down. I'll start off by killing Winston. I'll get my Demogorgon to get him. Then I'll take Frances when the time is right. Three, two, one! I make my move. I have got him. Time to get the rest.

After some time, I killed a lot of people. Then this kid, Gary, tried to defeat me. They didn't defeat me but they got Winston back.

Lola Williams (12)
Alderbrook School, Solihull

FAMILY DINNER...

"Mmmm!"

Peppa inhaled the fresh smell of the juicy meat that Mommy Pig was frying downstairs. Without warning, Peppa tugged George's arm, dragging him to the kitchen.

With a cunning grin plastered on her face, Mommy Pig locked intense eye contact with the children. Their plates were filled with greasy, fatty bacon. The eyes of Peppa and George lit up to see this sumptuous meal before them.

After polishing the remains of the bacon off, along with Mommy and George, Peppa realised Daddy Pig wasn't there. With hesitation, Peppa looked outside to see a pile of bones.

"Mommy, where's Daddy?"

Verity Jones (13)
Aldridge School, Aldridge

THE UNDERWORLD

He climbed the tree at the speed of lightning. No sound, just the call of the wolves in the distant valley and the song of the birds flying around. When he finally got to the tree top, he was in the open and yet he was hidden. Nobody could climb a tree in less than thirty minutes, except for Jo... Never mind.

He jumped down with a leopard's skill. Suddenly, a shining figure appeared and grabbed the boy's shoulder, pulling him into another realm. The Underworld. A place where souls chose what to do. The place of Hades' dark rule.

Antonina Maciejewska (12)
All Saints Catholic High School, Sheffield

THE FREAK

I never really got a chance to make a name for myself. I had always been labelled the 'freak'. So when the principal's assistant barged into my English lesson asking for me, I wasn't exactly the happiest.

I'd just like to clarify that I absolutely despise this school and everyone inside. 'Just change schools!' Maybe tell that to the genius who thought it was a good idea to have the only other school in the city an hour away from where we live. But if only this school knew what I had in plan for them in the last term...

Fatima Shad (13)
All Saints CE Academy, Ingleby Barwick

CINDERELLA'S STALKER

Once upon a time, there was a beautiful girl called Cinderella. She lived in a small town; everyone adored her. The prince loved Cinderella so he threw a ball for her to attend. Even though he loved her, he had an evil plan to keep her to himself.

On the night of the ball, Cinderella dressed up all pretty and the prince loved her dress. Finally, after everyone had left but Cinderella, the prince laid sticky tar on the stairs. She ran out and stuck to the floor. He kept her forever.

The good guys aren't always what they seem.

Evelyn Mallett (12)
All Saints CE Academy, Ingleby Barwick

DAY IN THE LIFE OF A MINION

One Minion day, I go to gather my scrumptious bananas. All until my master calls me down. "Hi there, Gru." He responds to me in this weird and strange language.

Ten minutes later all I know is I'm on some weird rocket. Fridays are the best. We have parties and have some cold drinks which I don't know and some cold food which I don't know.

Sometimes I think to myself about when I'm older. I want to be able to order people around to test machines, get me drinks, food and bananas. I love bananas so much.

Elliot Rome (13)

All Saints CE Academy, Ingleby Barwick

LITTLE DEAD RIDING HOOD

My parents once told me a story. When I swiftly fall asleep, I wake in front of this door with a twisted handle. It slowly creaks open. I stand, frozen with fear. I hear a diabolical, horrific, ghostly growl behind me. Chills crawl up my spine. Adrenaline courses through my veins.

I run forwards and fly up the stairs, feeling it behind me. I lunge into a room, a bedroom. I sigh with relief then I see Grandma's husk. It manifests before me, grabs me and cackles. I scream as I'm engulfed by it and then... I don't wake up.

Matthew Easby (13)

All Saints CE Academy, Ingleby Barwick

ORPHAN

One night there was a little saddened strange girl sitting on an orphanage bed. She was eager to find a family but no one wanted her.

One day a couple came to look for a child. Today was her day. They wanted to adopt her.

As she strolled to the car, waving at the other kids, the couple noticed something odd. She was very hairy. What they didn't know was that she was no little girl, she was a monster.

After a while, they noticed more unusual behaviour. She was hurting her brother and sister. She was a psychopath.

Eleisha Delapanosta (13)
All Saints CE Academy, Ingleby Barwick

MOTHER NATURE'S FEELINGS

I suddenly found my people on my planet suffering. A new virus? This virus is called Coronavirus. It has only been around for twenty years and it has killed millions of my people. I was in pain seeing people suffer along with people littering and getting too warm. It hurt seeing people in pain and dying... I needed to help. My people were in pain and suffering but I was also suffering from climate change, litter and this virus and war.
I hope this tragedy ends soon so I can feel better again. What will happen to me next?

Rachel White (13)
All Saints CE Academy, Ingleby Barwick

THEM

Thundering clouds covered the sky like the world was caving in. The wind howled and trees swayed. Then I could feel it. They were coming. I could feel my body start to shake with coldness. I was so scared.

Suddenly it hit me. A sigh of pain left my cold blue lips and I know it sounds made up, but I felt a happy feeling. But then it all went black. Darkness. Absolute darkness. Was I dead? Then I heard voices. Out-of-this-world voices. Mumbling to one another. And then silence. Nothing. My eyes opened. It was them.

Hanna Barnes (13)
All Saints CE Academy, Ingleby Barwick

HER LAST NAP

The smell of the porridge was scrumptious and mouth-watering, so much so that her nose drew her into the cottage and to the porridge. After she had gobbled that down, her stomach was full and she was sleepy. She wandered up the stairs and managed to find a cosy and comfortable bed.

A sudden noise awakened her that came from the owners. She tried to keep out of sight but then panic came rushing to her mind, realising it was great big bears and they weren't amicable. She was ripped apart like a piece of bread.

Jessica Purvis (13)
All Saints CE Academy, Ingleby Barwick

WILLOW AND THE THREE BAD BOYS

Once upon a time, there was a girl called Willow. She had two men that she liked and they liked her back. She didn't know who to pick. She had a talking dog called Poppi that didn't like one of them, his name was Sam. But the one the dog wanted her to date was a really strong, ripped guy who got all the girls. His name was Nick. He was so hot.
One day Nick and Willow were out at the Metro Centre going shopping then Willow saw this really tall, handsome man called Ben and they bearhugged.

William Stansil (12)
All Saints CE Academy, Ingleby Barwick

FROZEN INFERNO

It was a normal day until I became really frustrated with Elsa and lashed out, causing Arendelle to be covered with fire. I had to run away, I just had to. I heard Elsa tried to freeze the fire but of course, it was far too strong even for her.

I had nowhere to live so I created a haunted inferno house. It was epic! I knew I had to get rid of Elsa but I didn't know how without making it suspicious. Luckily, Elsa came to my house. Perfect! I did it! Nobody knows the truth about me!

Georgia Walker (13)
All Saints CE Academy, Ingleby Barwick

CLOUDY

Today was a normal day. The sun was out opposite me and I was shining bright with no rain inside of me whatsoever. Suddenly I felt rain inside of me and I knew it was time. I let free at last. Water bucketed from me like it was a stormy night and I lay my rain onto the person I hated the most. The person that polluted my home and made my life a misery.

He was mortified. He knew it was me by the way the rain was and I was so proud. He never polluted ever again.

Lola McAskill (12)

All Saints CE Academy, Ingleby Barwick

HOW PLANKTON STOLE THE KRABBY PATTY RECIPE

At last, I have finally stolen the Krabby Patty recipe. This is how I did it. So first I got a chainsaw and made a little hole so I could fit through it. Then I got into the room with the safe in it. Then I got a picklock and twisted the safe open. Then I had to climb over some money and then I had to hide away from Mr Krabs. Then I got the bottle with the recipe in it then had to run out of the Krusty Krab and run back over to the Chum Bucket.

Ethan Shepherd (13)
All Saints CE Academy, Ingleby Barwick

THE DAY THAT CHANGED EVERYTHING

It was just a normal day, riding my bike and going to the shops. But then everything changed. When I was paying for the milk, I heard a loud bang. I looked out of the shop window and the entire sky was red. Car alarms were going off. People were running. I stared up to find some sort of robot laser cutting the earth apart. There was nothing I could do.

I thought of a plan. I attached sticky bombs to the robot's legs and blew the robot up. The sky returned to normal, people were cheering and clapping.

Campbell Menzies (14)
Balerno Community High School, Balerno

THE EXTINCTION OF THE IMPOSTERS

The crew were doing their tasks as normal but there were imposters on the ship. The crew got really scared and worried but they had to finish their tasks. The imposters were a kind of alien on the verge of extinction because their crewmates were testing on them. So a few imposters escaped the testing room and made a plan to kill all of the crewmates to be able to free the other imposters and save them from extinction. They went back to their home planet to repopulate their planet. They also learned how to protect their planet from crewmates.

Jamie Ward-Moore (13)
Berwickshire High School, Langtongate

TWISTED FAMILY

Adeline and Briella were twins in a famous family. They were only expecting one baby, Adeline. Briella was unexpected and had a limb length discrepancy. Since they didn't want Briella and her medical condition they pushed her away and locked her in a room for years and years. Once Briella was 13 she didn't see anyone, the only thing she saw was the darkness. Eventually, she lost her mind. She broke out and decided to hunt down her sister...

Chloe Penman (14)
Berwickshire High School, Langtongate

FRANKENSTEIN'S GINGERBREAD MAN

It was then that my fantasies had finally become a reality. I watched my creation, generated from purely gingerbread and other irresistible confectioneries, be infused with life. I admired it emerging from its previously immortalised sleep. However, this creation didn't appear to replicate the beauty I'd dreamt of. Gradually the wretched creature attempted to reach for me, its grotesque finger crumbling ominously. Instantly repulsed, I clutched its arm, trying to disassemble the creation. However, only succeeding in breaking off the forearm. Terror drowned its face, and before I could stop it, it fled out the door, running into the distance.

Marcy Metcalfe (13)
Bristol Brunel Academy, Speedwell

CRIMINALS AND CREATURES

I sat down. "What-" A shower of bricks covered the room as my interrogatee furrowed her eyebrows. As the dense cloud of dust disappeared, three figures emerged. Their brown fur enveloped their bodies and livid growls escaped their mouths. In total silence, they snatched my blonde interrogatee and held her firmly as she struggled. They looked at me menacingly and the tallest one snarled, "Not a word." With fear for my life, I nodded before they ran out of the room onto the street. I saw one bear scratch the victim. I suddenly realised who it was... it was Goldilocks.

Kabir Saboor (13)

Bristol Brunel Academy, Speedwell

CORALINE

It was morning, Coraline awoke from her slumber. She shifted towards her bags on the floor - she was moving. Her parents carried things from the home into the car. Once done, they drove towards their new home.

Several hours later they had reached their new destination. Coraline's parents emptied the car. As Coraline trailed through the empty house she came to a room. A machete lay next to a door. She smiled and stabbed her parents, leaving lifeless bodies. She made her way towards the door and greeted her other mother that awaited. "I did what you said," she smiled.

Kairah-Essiene Pochot Fleming (13)

Bristol Brunel Academy, Speedwell

DREAMS COME TRUE

My dreams had come true! I'd woken up, I couldn't stop smiling. I could hear Romeo's sweet voice. I quickly got up to find him. I got closer to the forest and could hear a lot of commotion. It was Romeo and Tybalt - they were screaming and shouting at each other. I was very reluctant to get involved because I didn't want to be injured by their swords. After a few minutes I shouted, "Romeo, Tybalt, enough!" They both turned, dropping their swords. Both were gobsmacked to see me. I dusted the cobwebs off my dress. "I'm back," I exclaimed.

Evie Williams (13)
Bristol Brunel Academy, Speedwell

A TWISTED CINDERELLA STORY

As Cinderella arrived at the ball, mockingly she repeated the words her mother had said. "Be back by midnight or there will be consequences." People surrounded her as she walked into the ballroom, pairs of eyes glaring at her. Not long after she arrived she sat alone as no one wanted to dance with her. She wanted to disobey her mother by going back after midnight so she stayed till 11:59pm. Smirking as the clock struck midnight until unexpectedly someone swooped her up and took her to a dark room. Suddenly, a scream echoed through the building as blood spilled.

Karis Cunningham (13)
Bristol Brunel Academy, Speedwell

MISS BELL'S MURDER MOST UNLADYLIKE

I couldn't believe my eyes. It was all true, I finally found out Mrs Grant's hidden secret. Unfortunately, she had found out mine as well. Petrified, I could hear her footsteps approaching. Out of the corner of my eye, the shadow was becoming greater. *Thud!* The sound of Mrs G pushing me off the gym balcony. I pictured her gasping in horror as she hurried outside. Luckily, the gymnastics mat broke my fall. I couldn't move and my body was aching. Then, Hazel came and I pretended to be dead. Hazel looked like she was vomiting. This isn't the end...

Tierra Ferguson (11)
Bristol Brunel Academy, Speedwell

CINDERELLA AND THE WITCH OF SNOWY MOUNTAIN

The plan was in motion. I walked out into our yard, dressed in a scabby dress and slip-ons. In the distance, a vibrant woman stood as if she was a statue. "Hello," I called.
She turned around. "Want a lift?" She blew some smoke out her mouth. "Suppose you could do with a dress as well." I nodded. She took a crooked-looking wand and shook it. Within seconds a red dress appeared on me.
"Thank you!" I cried.
"Come on then."
All that is left of me today are my remains outside the ball I was going to...

Connie Tripp (12)
Bristol Brunel Academy, Speedwell

THE CROWN

I grabbed his hand and got on the boat. I looked at him confused. Why was he so quiet? "Are you okay?" I questioned.

"Rapunzel I'm sorry." Before I could even reply I suddenly felt a burning sensation. I looked down to see he had plunged a dagger in my stomach. I slowly looked back at him. "Where's the crown?" he demanded. One single tear rolled down my cheek. It wasn't the physical pain that hurt me. It was a sharpened dagger carving out the part of me that trusted until all that remained was a fragment of light left.

Junaidah Phiri (13)
Bristol Brunel Academy, Speedwell

MOTHER?

I sat in my dull tower, searching for information on my mother. Who was she? "There must be something about her in one of these books," I muttered to myself. After a while of flicking through the pages and scattering books all over the room, something finally caught my eye; a newspaper from 2001. That's the year I was born. I picked up the crumpled paper before me and read it out loud. 'Royal baby stolen from crib in the middle of the night. Kidnapper suspected to be Hecate Gothel.' Tears flooded my eyes as the realisation struck me. Mother?

Faith Manu-Cato (12)
Bristol Brunel Academy, Speedwell

JULIET AND ROMEO

I have never even liked him. He was just another useless toy I played with. Romeo Montague, a stupid little teenage boy fooled by love. I did have a plan though, a plan that would forever end my one and only problem, he would be a thorn in my side no longer. "Juliet!" a familiar voice called to me. I took from my drawer Friar's potion. Hastily, I lay down, closing my eyes. "Juliet! I'm coming... What have you done?" He took the potion from my hand and drank it. "See you soon love."
I opened my eyes and smirked.

Galisia Svetlomirova (13)
Bristol Brunel Academy, Speedwell

SNOW WHITE'S TRUTH: THE HUNTER'S TAKE

She was isolated in a kingdom where everyone knew her name. She cried but her tears were hidden. Her 'darling' prince knew but did nothing to stop her pain.
They carried in the box. Her once iconic white skin was now deathly pale. Her once crimson lips seemed drained. Lifeless. I thought back to her, an innocent kid robbed of childhood. I wished I hadn't spared her. That I'd let her misery end at the evil queen's hands on her heart, but instead she had to smile whilst holding the hand of her thief. So she ended the pain herself.

Madinah Hussain (13)
Bristol Brunel Academy, Speedwell

LITTLE DEVIL HOOD

One evening, Devil Hood was walking to her grandma's house as she usually would. Little did she know, she was being approached by a fat slobbery obese wolf. She didn't know, nor was she aware. She was listening to Ed Sheeran's 'Shape of You'. The wolf got closer to the point it was right in front of her. In horror, she screamed as loud as she could. She battled him to the ground and eventually killed him, but then found a zipper that led inside the wolf. It was Grandma! She didn't know what to do. She'd just killed Grandma!

Tayla Boulton-Treharne (12)
Bristol Brunel Academy, Speedwell

NOISES

Loud thumps were heard underneath my room, piercing through the soothing whispers of my curtains. What could possibly be the issue at this hour? I trudged my legs through the narrow passageway, the cold air dense on my pale cheeks. The pulsing lantern I held in the palm of both my hands revealed a carved oak door which I then opened. A candle lay on a desk, its last flame on the verge of descending into the air. Under my feet, fresh drops of splattered blood flowed in-between the wrinkles of the wooden flooring. However, the door was untouched...

Alesia Rus (12)
Bristol Brunel Academy, Speedwell

MESSI'S LAST UCL FINAL

Istanbul lightened as Leo stepped onto the pitch in Madrid. He was anxious and his heart went fast. Many of the start players were crying, so was Leo. "Come on guys, we have won so many UCLs together, let's win one more," said Messi, motivating his team to win this game.

The game was kicked off and the tension was all around the stadium. Bayern were through on goal with Sadio Mane and then he cut it back for Lewandowski fo 0-1. Then Modri equalised with a good side-foot goal. Messi got a free kick... He stepped up... Real won!

Mario Toshev (12)
Bristol Brunel Academy, Speedwell

A SLEEPING BEAUTY

I strode slowly to her bed where she lay still. As I stood above her I remembered a true love's kiss would awaken my sleeping beauty. So that was precisely what I gave her. As I lifted my head I waited for her to awaken... nothing. I pondered it, then kissed her again... but still... nothing. I tried more until my lips throbbed. She lay there, teasing life with unconsciousness. I sat in disarray whilst contemplating lending her more kisses. I walked round the pungent bed and paused. An identity tag loosely hugged her rotting toe. Wrong girl!

Laura Harrison-Algaba (14)
Bristol Brunel Academy, Speedwell

THE THREE LITTLE PIGS

The first day out of the woods didn't go as planned as I stumbled upon some pigs, which would be a good thing but they escaped into some houses they built. This was starting to get annoying. As I walked up to the first house to what I thought was the youngest pig's house, I realised it was made out of straw. Nothing I couldn't take down. I used my sharp claws, slowly taking down the poorly manufactured walls to reveal a pig's tail quickly escaping into the darkness of the night, but I quickly grabbed the shivering small tail.

Jaydon Broadley (13)
Bristol Brunel Academy, Speedwell

ROMEO AND JULIET

Nobody knew the truth about me. They still don't. My plan was in motion and nobody could stop me now. Romeo and Juliet were made for each other, but I needed her. Me, a mute man who wanted a schoolgirl. Unusual, right? So that's when the messaging started. I had gotten so obsessed with threatening them and knowing where they lived made it even better. They didn't know me then, and you don't need to know me now.

Months went by, they started catching on but by the time they knew it was me, it was over for them.

Asma Ali (12)
Bristol Brunel Academy, Speedwell

WHAT DID THIS?

I awoke. Nobody else had. I stood up and walked over to my friend's bed. I watched as blood oozed out of her mouth. Everyone I knew was dead. I went outside and everything was silent. *How?* I thought. Why was I the only one left? I closed my eyes as tears fell down my face. This was it. I could run away from the lab. The hellhole. I looked down, stepping in blood. Other people's innocent blood. I stepped over the human race. *What did this?* I thought. I reached into my pocket and pulled out a knife...

Vince Taylor (12)
Bristol Brunel Academy, Speedwell

RETRIBUTION

They didn't know. Dumbledore was a liar. That man was to open the world of magic to earth. Although he's now dead I believe the boy, the one with the bolt, is to carry on that malevolent plan. As you read this I am now gone... but not dead. I managed before the blast reached me to divert some of my soul into another creature. A raven to be precise. I will gather followers and friends while regaining my power to bring back my body and finally crush those who wronged me. I'll stop them before it's too late.

Muhammad Athar (12)

Bristol Brunel Academy, Speedwell

THE WOLVES

As I stumbled through the forest, I heard a rustle of leaves in the distance. The sound got louder and louder as I travelled further into the forest. I stepped as soft as a feather and slowly proceeded my adventure. A large, hungry pack of wolves pounced out of the shadows and growled in hunger. I placed my basket down and pushed it to one of the wolves. The wolves tore the basket to bits and their eyes zoomed right towards me. I ran but my scrawny legs couldn't match their speed. Next minute, I was ripped to shreds.

Brody Carter-Edwards (12)

Bristol Brunel Academy, Speedwell

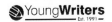

THE FINAL THOUGHTS OF THANOS

Nobody knew the truth about me and that truth is I miss Gamora. Greatly. We were all on the battlefield. I was winning when all of a sudden I saw my dear daughter. I suddenly stopped and rushed in to hug her. My biggest regret was leaving her. I ran in and fell face first as I realised it was one of Black Panther's sister's fake visual gadgets. That's when I figured out I was going to fail. Soon after, Thor came in and stole my only power, the glove. There was nothing left in me. That's when I died.

Danaya Georgieva (13)
Bristol Brunel Academy, Speedwell

MAXIMUM RIDE

I couldn't believe it. The people who were working as scientists were putting poison in Angel's arm. I sprang up with powerful wings and I went into all the scientists and made them fall. I went straight for Angel and carried her out. I saw the scientist that had raised us, me and the others. I was raging. Out of frustration, I sprang into the air and out a big window. I felt something shoot in my wings. I fell straight into deep water, it was freezing. I couldn't get out and fly. This was the end...

Aya Nariman (12)
Bristol Brunel Academy, Speedwell

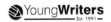

DWARVES ATTACK

That was the day of sorrow and grief... A loud cry was heard as the fire blazed, arrows had no effect on the bloodthirsty creature, its scales shining brightly. A brave man stared in terror before he was turned to dinner. His efforts would not go in vain, as now we had an opening. The archers fired and the beast fell. We had some time to grieve for the ones we had lost, but we had to prepare for the next attack. When would this nightmare ever end? We didn't have time to ask, the next attack was incoming...

Lukas (12)
Bristol Brunel Academy, Speedwell

THE THREE LITTLE PIGS

Sprinting after the two of them, running into a brick house. I ran up to it, trying to blow it down. I heard the door lock. Suddenly, an idea popped into my head. I walked round, hoping there was a back door. Fortunately, there was, so I jumped the fence and quietly walked in. Creeping around the house, I heard them snorting at each other. It was coming from the stairs. I tiptoed up the stairs. I passed a room and saw wolf guts everywhere. I ran in to find the three pigs in the middle of the crime scene.

Phoebe Jones (13)
Bristol Brunel Academy, Speedwell

ROMEO'S SAVIOUR

My dreams had come true. I woke up knowing that Romeo was going to drink the poison. Luckily, I had woken up in time to try to stop him. I ran over to the Capulet town where Romeo was. I saw the potion through the window. Romeo was awake, thinking about the potion. As I looked through the window Romeo grabbed the potion. I started to get worried. As quick as I could I ran in and took the potion out of Romeo's hand, knowing the effects of it. I was glad I'd saved Romeo. I told Romeo the effects.

Oliver Jobbins (13)
Bristol Brunel Academy, Speedwell

BEAUTY IS PAIN

Every year there would be a forest that I would go to due to the flowers that I would see, but whenever I was there, for every step I took I would hear a squeal and for each breath I took I would cough, but never thought much of it. One day I went on my yearly forest walk but this time was different. I coughed way more and felt more breathless until the moment I went home. I collapsed into my mother's arms while a wave of blood poured out of my mouth with beautiful flowers painting the blood.

Eva-Raquel Jurca Latienda (12)
Bristol Brunel Academy, Speedwell

THE NEW FARM

After a long journey, I arrived at another farm as I was kicked out and betrayed by the other pigs. At first I was not accepted but later on the other animals at the new farm found out that I had an education. After a tough sleep at the new farm, I limped to where all of the other animals were. I realised that the rest of the animals were a lot nicer to me. I introduced the plan of a windmill and explained every advantage of it. I finally got to make the windmill without my idea being taken.

Ibrahim Riaz (13)
Bristol Brunel Academy, Speedwell

FRANKENSTEIN'S MONSTER

I have to tell you, I didn't know why some crazy guy brought me to life, but I knew I wasn't going to live in his grimy lab. Naturally, I woke up and destroyed everything in the room. He ran away like a little baby. I found him and pummelled him fatally. Then, I ran far away and people were fascinated by my appearance. Soon after, I became the star of my very own movie. Everyone who sees me screams in joy, but they always run away when I try to get close to say hello to them.

Solomon Hylton (13)
Bristol Brunel Academy, Speedwell

SUPERMAN SAVES THE WORLD

It is a dark, dark night. Superman flies fast through the clouds. One baby zombie is eating the flesh of one innocent person at a time to create an army. More zombies come out from the wet soil.

Banana, the huge wolf, is Superman's pet. The wolf is sleeping on Superman's bed peacefully, listening to music. Suddenly, a diamond 'S' appears in the black sky. Banana attacks the baby zombie. Then, ten thousand more! Superman and Banana work together to fight and win.

Ryan Sutton-Lucas (12)
Bristol Brunel Academy, Speedwell

THE MYSTERIOUS HAWK

It was an early sunny morning in December. A young man woke up and went for his run. He was on his run when he saw something pop in the window, but it was nothing. So he carried on. As he got back home he took a shower to cool down. The young man heard his doorbell ring so he got up and answered the door but nothing was there. There it was again. A bird rushed through and brushed past him. It was a hawk sat on top of the stone looking very tired and scared.

Danny Bennett (13)
Bristol Brunel Academy, Speedwell

THE WOLF'S REGRETS

After I came out that house, I realised I'd made a grave mistake. I angered her, I ate her grandma. I may not be trustworthy, but I really didn't mean it this time. I was just hungry. She'll try to find me now. I can't stay hidden in the woods. I have to hide. What's that sound? Oh no... she's here. Is that an axe swinging? No, no... where's a hiding spot? She's coming closer... I wish I wasn't stuck in this wolf form.

Anisah Mulk (13)
Bristol Brunel Academy, Speedwell

RED

Werewolves... myth or real?

There was once a girl, Riding Hood, but this is not any ordinary fairy tale with a happy ending, so sit back if you are uncomfortable and I'll begin.

Hood never really felt like she belonged anywhere. Why you might ask? Well, she was a werewolf! Her grandma made sure of that from the day she was born and since then Hood had planned to kill her.

Grandma gathered all the townsfolk each day to torture her, for she was not of this world, but that scared them into madness. Hood never forgave and never forgot!

Matilda Unsworth (15)
Bury CE High School, Haslam Brow

NOT-SO-HAPPILY EVER AFTER

'Happily ever after' isn't always as it seems. Given a poisoned apple by a witch, on my deathbed and awakened by the kiss of a prince. I was sent off into the sunset hoping to get a new life with a heroic prince but my happily ever after is a misery. I'm fifteen years old, a fine girl named Snow White. My prince is my captor, 32 years of age. I work every day and am punished every night. I sometimes wish the apple had killed me off. It would be better to have died than live this horrible hell.

Charlotte Plant (13)
Bury CE High School, Haslam Brow

FINDING BARRACUDA

"You have brought shame to our kind. Now everyone in the world loves clownfishes and they hate barracudas. If you hadn't eaten that clownfish, we'd still be fine. Now go. We don't want you."

The barracuda could still remember the words his friends and family said to him. All he did was eat a clownfish and clownfish eggs, now everyone hates him. He didn't understand what he had done wrong, yet he felt regret and shame. He wanted help from the other fish, but they all ran from him. So he decided to hide away from everybody in the deep...

Amos Leung

Cambourne Village College, Cambourne

THE WANTED SISTER

A couple of weeks ago, I was wandering through the streets and saw posters of a wanted person everywhere. I heard sirens everywhere. I looked at the poster again. It was me! I was super confused, I hadn't done anything wrong. Everything went dark, I woke up in the hospital with doctors, police and my parents surrounding me. I got taken away and was questioned. My parents were there to back me up, but anyway, that's what I thought... They got me sent to prison. I was fuming.

I wondered where Cinderella was. Was she the one behind all this?...

Harriet Foggo (12)
Cambourne Village College, Cambourne

THE GLASS SLIPPER THAT DIDN'T FIT

Cinderella tried to wriggle free from her stepmother. Suddenly, a swarm of pain rushed over her. The chilling air hit her freshly-cut toes, unbearable burning pain. She could no longer feel or see anything. She woke up lying on the floor, trying to remember how she had got there. She looked at her feet and it all came rushing back to her. Rags covered her foot, sopping wet with blood. She screamed. Where once were her toes and heels, were now exposed veins and dried blood. She had to look away. Now, the glass slipper will never fit.

Isabella Blythe (13)

Chichester Free School, Bognor Regis

A GANG ESCAPE

I woke up in an abandoned room. Dust fell from the ageing roof. I coughed. The noise echoed through the empty chamber of a cell.

"So you're awake," an old lump groaned from the corner.

"Yes," I replied, rubbing my eyes violently.

"Where am I?" I wondered out loud.

"You're in a hospital," he groaned again.

"A hospital?" I yelled.

I was captured by a gang earlier today. They took me there.

"That's what they do," he said, suddenly sounding serious. "They bring us here, so *they* get us!"

Before I could speak, I heard a crash outside...

Nate Barnes (13)
Clifton High School, Clifton

THE REAPER

Danny sucks the wet end of a cigarette, tapping his hand on the steering wheel. Wisps of Maggie's hair whip around from the rolled-down windows. Burnt cedar wafts on the wind and night stretches beyond the oak trees lining the old country road. Occasionally, the truck bumps. When it does, the heavy body in the bed bumps too.

Maggie says, "I love this song," turning up the volume to drown it out. The pale tan line around her ring finger glows in the moonlight. She takes Danny's hand and sings, "Come on baby, don't fear the reaper. I'm... the reaper!"

Louis Watts (13)
Clifton High School, Clifton

THE CAR ACCIDENT

Mike woke to flashes of red and blue flooding through his blinds. It was the early hours of the morning. He already knew what the police were going to say from the grim looks on their faces. Mike was leaning over the banister as his mum was talking to the officers. He could only make out a couple of words: "Dad", "Accident", "Dead", "I'm sorry." As he stumbled back to his room, he couldn't help shedding a tear down his face. As he came down, his mum told him the unfortunate news. But suddenly, a familiar voice called out...

Harrison Taylor (12)
Clifton High School, Clifton

HOT-CROSSED BOMBS!

All across the world, volunteers planted bombs. Where? In shops, schools, official buildings, houses and wherever else they could. Every time global temperatures rose by 1°C, the bombs went off, each degree worse than the last. At 2°C, the Eiffel Tower crushed Paris. At 3°C, the Taj Mahal crumbled in on itself. Last time at 4°C, the White House turned soot-black. Companies sprung up for betting on the next landmark to fall. People had won millions. Jack walked along his street. He felt it before he saw it. 10 Downing Street disappeared, along with the PM!

Andrew Carter (13)
Clifton High School, Clifton

THE WILLOW MAN

The trees swayed. In the wood barn, the fire crackled and grey smoke flowed out of the chimney. The Willow Man sat on his chair staring at the picture of his victim. His eyes set on the details: *'Caroline, 28'*. His bloodstained axe in one hand, a prosthetic in the other. His rotten body stood up and turned to the door. Caroline heard a knock at her window. She turned. A rotten face stared at her. She screamed. A man outside heard the faint sound of an axe chopping. "Maybe they're cutting willow in there?"

Sam Motherwell (13)
Clifton High School, Clifton

THE HUMANITY CRISIS

Long ago in the year 2577, I, Mephiles, decided to build a time machine to destroy all humans. Some may say I'm a hero, but most would say I'm a villain. Anyway, as I travelled to the past - aided by my magnificent invention - I realised that the biodiversity on Earth could thrive without evil humans, and so I crafted a weapon, known by people as a gun, that could and would only end the lives of humans. There was no way of stopping me! As such, I saved Planet Earth and travelled back to my time in the year 2577.

Alfie England (13)
Clifton High School, Clifton

FORGIVEN?

After the curse had lifted we were unfrozen. My sister began to apologise. Although this is what I had longed for I couldn't help but feel anger, after all she had ruined my life. She was perfect, everyone loved her. I looked into her eyes and she looked into mine. Everyone was surrounding us at this point, I saw the hatred in their eyes whilst looking at me. It irked me how they all expected me to forgive her as if she hadn't made my life a living hell all these years. Although upset, I had my long-awaited dream. Revenge.

Alicia Davies (13)
Co-Op Academy Bebington, Bebington

STEREOTYPES OF THE SHARK

Nobody knows the truth about me. All they know is how vicious and evil I am. They all prejudge me because of my kind and how it is stereotypical. Whenever I see someone it's an instinct to attack and kill. One time when I was going about my day, I saw a person who was trying to get fish. *Bang!* My instinct snapped then I chased him. He was too slow. Nobody heard of him ever again. I felt terrible but nothing can be done. It's finished now. I swam back home with my kids.

Kieran Scott (14)

Co-Op Academy Bebington, Bebington

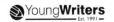
SLEEPING IN THE DARK

I woke up in the woods. *How did I get here?* I thought. Then it hit me. My sister tried to kill me last night. *She did all this because the prince is in love with me,* I thought.

"Finally, you're awake," I heard someone say.

I turned to see who it was.

"Well, well, well, look who it is. Hello sister," I said as she pulled a wand out. "Really? Who are you? Harry Potter?" I said as I pulled my sword out. "Come on, it takes two to tango," I said to her...

Anya Williams (12)
Coedcae School, Llanelli

CHARLIE AND THE NO RETURNERS

Willy Wonka announced the five golden tickets and my grandson won! The experience of being in the presence of Wonka was amazing. Along with Charlie, my grandson, there were four other children. I only remember Violet. Maybe that's because she blew up from the chewing gum. We warned her to stop chewing but she didn't listen! Just like all the others... The longer we roamed through the factory, the quieter it got.

"Like I said, I didn't kill them officer, I'm innocent..."

Layla Esposito-Williams (13)

Coedcae School, Llanelli

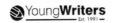
SNOW WHITE AND THE SEVEN DEVILS

"We must kill her, she cannot live!"
Snow White came across a lovely cottage with some really kind dwarves... or so she thought.
The seven dwarves gained her trust the more time they spent together. Snow White came across a hidden mirror that revealed a huge secret. The dwarves wanted to kill her. She must run away. She got ready to leave but before she did, she needed food. She grabbed an apple. With just one bite, she fell into an eternal sleep.

Rojda Otag (13)
Coedcae School, Llanelli

THE SAVIOUR

A terrible war's been going on for months. I'm hiding in my cellar for shelter. The walls are shaking and the floor's vibrating. I only have a small window for light but I can hear everything. Bombs, gunfire, sirens wailing, people screaming for help and crying. Constant smell of smoke and heat from the flames. I'm terrified. I hope my family have found a safe place. Everything goes deadly silent. The door rattles, and in comes a figure holding a rifle. I hold my breath expecting the worst. The enemy soldier holds out his hand. "It's okay, you're safe now."

Zoë Thomson (13)
Cove School, Cove

GHOST

Once there was a girl called Sophie. One morning, she went into the forest to find some mushrooms. The trees were swaying in the breeze and the morning dew sparkled on the leaves. The mushrooms were in her secret spot in the middle of the dense wood. On the way home, Sophie got lost and heard the noise of branches breaking behind her. She stopped and looked around and saw a shadowy figure approaching her. She screamed as loud as she could but no one could hear her, except the shadowy figure looming over her, pointing the way out.

Sophie Thomson (12)
Cove School, Cove

PINOCCHIO, THE SIDE NOBODY HAS SEEN...

Pinnochio was an average human boy who lived with his father who was very ill. They were incredibly poor with no money to buy food so he started stealing. He would wake up early and sprint to the shops to steal food.

Pinocchio continued this until he eventually got caught by officers which got him caught by his dad. Later that night, he was visited by a fairy who told him, "If you steal again, I will curse you."

The next day, he stole again and again. The fairy had enough and turned him into a doll... for eternity...

Riley Conyon (13)
Craigroyston Community High School, Edinburgh

SNOW

I hurry as I pack my bags for soon I will be free. Disguised in nothing but rags for soon I will flee. A wonderful mother, they say, with eyes the colour of honey but is that true as I'm forced to obey as she uses me for money.
Snow White is my name for my skin is as white as snow. I am devoured by fame so I'm forced to stay low.
I'm greeted with an icy breeze as I step out to freedom. This opportunity I will seize as I step into the forest kingdom.

Judy Akhdier (13)
Craigroyston Community High School, Edinburgh

MY UNLUCKY FATE

On a foggy night a child, who didn't believe in anything magical, came across a dark gloomy castle. She walked inside holding her head in her hands. *Bang! Clap!* The lightning struck.

Some witches unfolded.

"We can see you, my child," they said one by one.

The girl stood there in fear, knees giving in, unable to move.

"We have something for you, my dear.

The girl's knees gave in and she fell to the floor. *Bang! Clap!* This time it wasn't the thunder.

"We warned you, we warned you..." they sang with a soothing voice.

I was that child...

Hannah May Warr (13)
Cyfarthfa High School Lower, Merthyr Tydfil

THE MOUSE AND THE FROG

A frog was chilling in the swamp as a mouse passed by.
The mouse saw the frog and said, "Hello there, you are
looking quite lonely. Do you want to be my friend?"
The frog replied, "Yes! Yes!" What is your name?"
The mouse said, "Jake. What is yours?"
The frog replied, "My name is Jayden."
"Are you hungry? I can get you some cheese if you want."
"What is cheese?" the frog said. "I have never had cheese,
all I've had is flies and bugs. Sure I would love to try
something like cheese."

Jayden Simons (13)
Cyfarthfa High School Lower, Merthyr Tydfil

A HERO WHO SAVED CHRISTMAS

I ran as fast as I could to save the decorations that had been stolen that once filled the town with joy.

"Hey! Stop!" I shouted as the villain ran away with the decorations.

He was running towards a mountain. I had to put my plan into motion. I threw my nets as he threw the decorations over the edge. The nets got there just in time. The net caught the decorations, saving them all. I pulled back the nets with the decorations in them.

As I put all the decorations back up, I was thanked by the town.

Ruby Jones (13)

Cyfarthfa High School Lower, Merthyr Tydfil

DESIRABLE GRU

Gru was a normal man, but he had a couple of tricks up his sleeve. He had no company in his life until he took a walk down his local neighbourhood. He saw a yellow-looking thing. He went up to it. It was digging through the bins. He picked it up. The yellow thing was called a Minion. It started speaking a weird language. It looked very cute. Its name was Bob. He took Gru to his base. There were 500+ more. They all hugged him together.

Reuben Lackman-Jones (13)
Cyfarthfa High School Lower, Merthyr Tydfil

UNGUARDED (FLUFFY'S SIDE OF THE STORY)

Who were these three children daring to disturb me? Each of my three noses sniffed them in turn: a boy with glasses, a girl with frizzy hair and a scruffy red-haired boy. I presented my best growl and snarl, ready to pounce. Suddenly, the sound of soothing music filled my ears. My body relaxed, my eyelids grew heavy and before I could react I was asleep. After, what felt like only a few seconds, I awoke to see the children disappearing through the trapdoor. I howled viciously. I had been so foolish. Now the Philosopher's Stone would be found.

Jonas Mullington (12)
Denstone College, Denstone

THE ONE WHO LOST HIS WAY

Everything was going good until the signal fire broke out. My fellow littluns ran for dear life. I'd stayed trying to fight the fire until I had been surrounded by the raging flames. I dropped to my knees, praying to God for mercy. Suddenly, the smoke got to me and I plummeted unconscious. When I woke up; I was confused. "Why hasn't anyone looked for me? Am I dead?" I was mentally and physically torn but I knew what had to be done. Soon after, I constructed my own shelter out of leaves and sticks. I'm on my own now.

Keatan Bagraith (15)
Denstone College, Denstone

JACK HOLDS THE POWER

Piggy was dead, I shouted and threw my spear. Ralph curled over. He hopelessly attempted to throw one back, before taking his last breath on the sand. I was in charge now, no one could stop me. I got to work making some laws. Any act of stealing or harm was punishable by death. Right after I had killed Ralph, a littlun pushed me. I used him as an example but people kept on stealing food, saying that they were hungry. I certainly wasn't so how could they be? Now it is just me. I set the rules, I'm powerful.

Seth Harrison (13)
Denstone College, Denstone

CINDER FELLA

It was a big day today. The postman came and dropped off two letters - one about the royal ball and the other was about a monster that had escaped. The god fairy came and gave Cinderella three wishes. Cinderella wished for a horse, carriage and a wonderful dress. Cinderella got to the ball and saw the prince. The monster was hiding in the bushes. The lights went out and everyone began screaming. The monster came out and started grabbing people. It picked Cinderella and she was never seen after that day. The prince looked for her every day.

Konrad Wilk (14)
Forres Academy, Forres

LITTLE DEAD RIDING HOOD

She knocked on the door, no answer. Lifting the latch, she slowly opened it. She made her way across the hallway, down the corridor to the sitting room. "Grandma," she whispered, getting scared. As she walked to the back of the house, she caught the glimpse of a shadow out of the corner of her eye. She turned, hearing the floorboards groan. The shadow was coming closer and she could now make out what it was... The creature slunk towards her - a villainous look plastered on its face. The only sound, her blood-curdling screams echoing throughout the house.

Maisie Gordon (13)
Gairloch High School, Gairloch

HANSEL AND GRETEL - FUGITIVES

"It was October 2nd, I was in Sainsbury's looking for bread when I saw Hansel and Gretel loitering around the bakery scoffing doughnuts before suddenly dashing away. After purchasing my baguette, I followed the trail of doughnut crumbs they'd carelessly left behind. It led me to Tesco where a crusty man waited.

"Way to go Kiddos!" he croaked. "Soon Sainsbury's won't exist and Tesco shall rule!"

"Whatever witch, just give us our dough!" Gretel replied.

He gave them money and they left. I immediately called the police which brings me to this interview and that is all I know!"

Emelia Maddocks (12)
Hazel Grove High School, Hazel Grove

TANGLED TO STRANGLED

"Rapunzel, let down your hair!" I called.

"Coming, Mother!" she replied. Her golden locks were swirled around her neck when she lifted her knife. "I know what you did," Rapunzel said.

She was going to cut her hair when I saw my chance... I couldn't let her lose her powers, I wouldn't survive. I grasped at the ends of her hair and pulled tight. She gasped and struggled, her face losing colour. Then she toppled from the tower and hit the ground with a thud. Her sky-blue eyes stared blankly but I stayed young.

"I'm sorry, dear," I said.

Georgia Brown (13)
Hazel Grove High School, Hazel Grove

ARENDELLE: THE LOST KINGDOM

Anna's body was frozen by Alsa's uncontrollable powers. Their kingdom began to hunt Elsa so she fled to her ice castle. Elsa's powers then faded due to Anna being dead and Elsa became stuck in her castle and she could no longer control the ice. She was stuck in her creation forever with nobody to bring back the four seasons. Arendelle, Anna and Elsa's kingdom, remained crystallised in ice and snow for eternity. Soon after Elsa's death, the citizens of Arendelle could not move, talk or even breathe. Even now, explorers search for the lost kingdom, yet nobody's been successful.

Emilia Twemlow (12)
Hazel Grove High School, Hazel Grove

PRINCE CHARMING'S LOVE

"I don't want to!" I explained.

"Prince Charming, you are soon to be a king, you need a wife and Cinderella is perfect!" Father yelled. "You shall meet her at the ball tonight, that's final!"

It was time, there she was. Cinderella ran to me and immediately introduced me to her mother. I couldn't care less about the conversation, instead I stared at the beautiful girl in the glimmering dress behind her. When she left the ballroom I snuck out and took her to my secret garden where we talked and talked all night. I had fallen in love. Oops.

Jessica Lancaster (12)
Hazel Grove High School, Hazel Grove

THE WHITE QUEEN'S ANNOUNCEMENT

I couldn't believe my eyes. The Queen of Hearts was defeated and my friends had defeated her. Whilst the town filled with laughter, the White Queen quietened them down for a special announcement. "I'd like to thank these courageous souls," she started.

Alice went up first, next was Hatter. Then the twins and finally, the white rabbit. I was sure it was my turn.

"I thank you all greatly!"

What? She forgot me? Me? I guided Alice, I spied for her, I did everything she asked and she forgot me!

"Not nice is it?" snarled the Red Queen.

Maggie Bradburn (13)
Hazel Grove High School, Hazel Grove

FROZEN

I'm Anna and I'm frozen with my sister Elsa hugging and trying to warm me.

Around a year later, I'm still frozen, watching my sister marrying my true love or so I thought as I'm not the one up there getting married to Kristoff!

My sister has been married for years now and they have five happy children. One is called Anna! Right now I'm still standing under the pictures on the wall.

My family has all passed away, only my niece Anna is alive, living in America. That's where I am now, stuck here like this forever and ever.

Faith Hughes (13)
Hazel Grove High School, Hazel Grove

THE THREE PIGS OF DEATH

The year is 2036, living in Texas, Rex (also known as Pig 3) was scouting for wolves and keeping in touch with his brothers Ronald and Reggie. Wolves have been said to be fearless and dangerous. As Reggie was scouting, he saw a wolf. Into the mic he shouted, "Every pig for themselves!" Ronald ran over to Reggie, his brother. He knocked on the door but that would be the last thing he did. Reggie shot him right in the head. "Ronald had a bit of an accident." "Okay," and then there lay Reggie, on the floor, killed by Rex.

Benji Fox (12)
Hazel Grove High School, Hazel Grove

ALADDIN WITH A TWIST

My dream had come true. I was the queen of the Arabian desert. I had to choose my husband. There were so many options but not many good ones. One specific man caught my eye, Jafar. Many months went by and it was finally my wedding day. "I do!" These two words changed my life forever. Walls came crashing down.

"Thank you for the power, now you must die!"

I let out a giant scream and ran for my life. I hid from the man I loved and promised myself it would be okay. Suddenly, I was found! "Argh! Help!"

Elicia Lewis (14)
Hazel Grove High School, Hazel Grove

A TRAVEL TO TWISTED TALES

Poof! I found myself peeping at the fairy godmother. I wanted to do something cruel. I jumped out, stole her wand and fled. I knew where Cinderella's house was. I felt I was at the time when the shoe fitting had nearly ended. I rushed to the house and came in perfect timing. I used the wanted to make the shoe fit a sister. Putting their foot in, they screamed with joy. I knew I had ruined Cinderella's life. I heard footsteps coming, the fairy godmother... I ran, I couldn't escape. I wish to go to a different story!

Raeesa Hossain (12)

Hazel Grove High School, Hazel Grove

TWISTED TALE

Once, a young teenager went on a quest with her bear mum when her mum started to act strangely. There was something wrong! Her eyes turned pitch-black. Merida started to get scared and ran in fear into the forest. Suddenly her mum went crazy and started to chase her. In fear, Merida hid herself in a long, deep cave. The bear stomped into the cave with her long claws. Merida was cornered. The bear growled loudly with Merida in the corner in fear. The bear had no hesitation. It quickly struck Merida. Sadly her face was scarred for life.

Merrily Maunder (13)
Hazel Grove High School, Hazel Grove

MY STORY

It all started when I was being nosy and stumbled across Coraline's room, after all, the Pink Palace has been empty for months. Then she woke up and followed me, she was like a sleeping zombie running after me. Finally I moved through the tunnel and you'll never guess what... she did too? Hasn't anyone taught this girl that if you had weird tunnels in your house leading to other worlds, don't go in them?! She crawled into the long tunnel. I felt guilty but I was glad as she gave me some cheese. Yum!

Jacob Newman (12)
Hazel Grove High School, Hazel Grove

THE WOLF'S CHALLENGE

I'll never forget when I, the little wolf, was being called weak by the three little pigs. "I bet you can't break into three houses that we make," they teased, but I disagreed. This was where the challenge began. The first house was made of straw so I got a leafblower and blew the house down. The second was made of sticks so I got some matches and burnt it to ashes. The third was made of bricks... I got a firework and blew the house up. The pigs went flying into the air and never came back.

Jasmine Heslin (12)
Hazel Grove High School, Hazel Grove

LITTLE RED KIDNAPPED

As Little Red Riding Hood was casually strolling to her grandma's house, in the blink of an eye, she was abducted by five people in an invisible flying van. They were flying through the sky and her time was coming to an end until a flicker of hope appeared. It was Grandma, she was wearing a jet pack and she disintegrated all of them with a rubber duck that was actually a ray gun. Then Little Red Riding Hood and her grandma flew back by jet pack. When they got home, they shared a delicious wolf pie.

Max Horley (12)
Hazel Grove High School, Hazel Grove

DIARY OF THE SMELLY KID

13th October 2043. It was a cold autumn day. Greg Heffley was in hospital recovering from a terrible car crash that he got into. But one day he saw a figure outside his window, and if he looked away it moved closer.

One day he got out of hospital and started to drive home, but as he was driving he noticed a car following him and he kept getting flashbacks which made him go crazy. Then it clicked. He noticed it was the same car and then he got into another car crash and ended up back in hospital.

Lacia Keay (11)
Hazel Grove High School, Hazel Grove

LITTLE BLUE WALKING COAT

Hello! I am Bailey. Yes, I am an elephant but I'm here to tell a tale. The tale of Little Blue Walking Coat. Her grandpa had sent her out for groceries. She went to Asda and that's also where she saw me! At first she was surprised, but then she started crying and screaming. Little Blue Walking Coat had called for her dad who was a zoo worker. I was taken to the zoo and put in this massive enclosure. But then I saw a monster. It was as small as a button but still as frightening as a mouse.

Grace Stonier (12)

Hazel Grove High School, Hazel Grove

TOM AND JERRY TWIST

One day the cat and the mouse's owner went out to dinner.
The mouse was eating food and then the cat stole the food
and made Jerry mad so he had to get his revenge. When the
cat went to drink the milk he had to do something so he
stole the milk and threw it out of the window. Then they said
to themselves, "Why do we always fight?"
The mouse said, "I don't know!"
So they called a truce and lived together forever with the
owner and never had a fight again.

Jamie Parlby (13)
Hazel Grove High School, Hazel Grove

MY TRUTH

Nobody knew the truth about me and that's how I killed my dad. One morning, my dad was running down the stairs in a war uniform. "Alfie, you're gonna have to look after yourself because I've been sent to war!" he said sadly. He reassured he would send letters but a year later, nothing had been sent. I was mad, I was so mad I wanted to kill my dad. I was tall for my age so I went to Germany by train and joined the war to get my dad. One night I found him and shot my dad.

Ellie McGregor (12)
Hazel Grove High School, Hazel Grove

WOLF

Wolf needs a new house. Three pigs walk up to Wolf and say, "You have lots of juicy bones." The pigs chase Wolf. They try to eat him. Wolf runs away from the vicious pigs. Wolf walks into the forest to hide. On the way, he finds his old friend Little Red Riding Hood and tells her about the pigs, then asks for help. They plan and get to work. After they go and hunt the three pigs. Wolf gets revenge on the three pigs and he wins. Wolf thanks Little Red Riding Hood.

Amy Atkins (12)
Hazel Grove High School, Hazel Grove

PAGON THE DRAGON

Like a bomb, they splashed into the river. The squirrel was soaked like a sponge. I saw them but as I was swooping down, they managed to get away. I waited and waited to see if they would try and come back but they didn't so I went to fly home when I saw them. They were hiding under a tree. I flew down but they managed to get away. I gave up and went straight home. I saw them again and I hid behind a big bush. I waited until they went past. I opened my mouth and bang!

Oliver Poole (12)
Hazel Grove High School, Hazel Grove

POISON IN THE COFFEE

The moment I married that woman I was only there for the money. Whilst she was saving her money to go to a weird mountain, I was slowly poisoning her. The day she died I took all the money and became rich, but the police showed up at my door so I used my chimney for a balloon escape route. I flew to the mountain and lived there with my dog, but one day my dog chewed on a string and all the balloons flew away so I couldn't get own and died of lack of food.

Jyles Hazlewood (11)
Hazel Grove High School, Hazel Grove

THE MONSTER HUNTER

I've been a monster hunter for a while now. As I was at the bar, something came crashing through the window and bit a man's hand off! It was a bat thing but it was normal. Then I went down to the swamp and a giant buffalo with arms rose from the lake, standing on two legs. Behind me I saw people screaming in the town. So I ran to my horse and rode to town. A giant snake rose from the sand! Everyone was shooting it and it went back to its slumber.

Joey Standard (12)
Hazel Grove High School, Hazel Grove

INCY WINCY SPIDER: THE HUMAN EATER!

It all started off in an old woman's house, down in the mouldy old overgrown basement. There, something scurried around and around, eating all the food and fertiliser. Later one day, the woman sadly didn't know that it had escaped through a pipe and had murdered and sucked on every adult's blood. It murdered them one by one until the whole town was gone and the only person left was the little old lady!

Oliver Kibble (13)

Hazel Grove High School, Hazel Grove

THE BIG BAD WOLF

Nobody knows the truth about me. I was trying to help my cubs, they call me 'The Big Bad Wolf' but I'm just 'Lonely Dad Wolf'. My wife was killed and I've cubs to care for. People are afraid of me but us wolves need to eat too so please don't hurt me. I just want to live my life like you guys, not a wolf. Everyone is afraid of us. Let me live my life and don't be mean to me. I'm not a big bad wolfie, just let me live my life. Let me live, please!

Selena Payne (12)
Helston Community College, Helston

HUNGRY, HOWLING

A wilted piece of spinach curls pitifully on my plate. I'm a wolf; I'm supposed to be eating prey. I can't survive off corn like my neighbour the chicken. But the propaganda being spread around has made killing to survive unacceptable and punishable by a life sentence.

People are already terrified of me. They think I will never change my hunting instincts. Perhaps they're right. No - they are right.

I'm a wolf. A wolf must kill to survive.

Matilda Stringer (13)

Helston Community College, Helston

WISH GRANTED

He descended into the room. "What are your three wishes?" the deceitful devil asked the imprisoned girl.

Cinderella replied, "For my first wish I want my stepmother to fall under the spell of an incurable plague."

"Wish granted," said the dark devil slyly.

"My next wish is to be free, not imprisoned."

"Wish granted," the devil said once again.

"My final wish is to return to my true form." Cinderella grinned wickedly at the devil.

"As you wish, my queen," said the devil as he snapped his fingers. Dark clouds enshrouded the room as lightning struck. "Welcome back, Queen Maleficent."

Aisha Fazeel (12)
Holy Trinity Catholic School, Small Heath

THE SHOE

There I was left on the floor alone after the boring ball. I felt worthless. I wanted revenge on her. I had a tingling feeling, a flash of light and I could move. It was a miracle. I was on a mission. I was coming for her. There she was in the distance. I tried to speed run. I was running out of breath but I put in all my effort. I got her. I jumped and hit her in the back of the leg. She tumbled to the ground. She got up. "Oh no, it's not my Cinderella."

Evelyn Houlden (13)
John Cabot Academy, Kingswood

BATTLE OF BOSWORTH FIELD

The plan was in motion. The battle was in full flow. The clash of metal against metal could be heard wherever you were. The lords had made their decision and they would pay for it. He fought his way through the soldiers, screaming in anger and pain, the blood crawling across the churned-up grass. He moved stealthily towards his opponent until he was so close he could have killed him with a dagger. He raised his sword and with a cry, he swung his blade through his enemy's throat. The battle was over. He'd won. Long live King Richard.

Ella Morgan Bailey (14)
King Alfred's Academy, Wantage

THE OTHER SIDE

After everything Bella had told her, Cinderella still believed the fake prince over her own sister...

Through the gates of her prison, Bella stared at a future that should've been hers. She'd worked scrubbing floors until her skin was raw; just to end up betrayed by her own family.

Cinderella had snatched Bella's perfectly planned happy ending, and now Bella stared with hate-filled eyes as the prince slid a ring onto Cinderella's finger. They had forced her to watch them, but little did they know, she held the key in her left hand and a knife in her right.

Nayana Pillay (15)
King Edward VI High School For Girls, Birmingham

CAPTAIN

I couldn't move I was too scared, the way my hands were violently shaking. The huge lump in the back of my throat felt like it would swallow me whole. I couldn't feel anything, I had blood head to toe. My knees had completely failed me. Yet, he was still on his feet, he kept on fighting. When he got knocked down, he got back up straight away. Luffy is stronger than I am, but that's why I look up to him. I know he will be the next Pirate King. He will find the one piece.

Lily Stevenson (14)
Kingsland School, Watersheddings

ANASTASIA

Suddenly, a loud knock echoed in the ornate entrance hall. A well-dressed stepmother answered the door and there stood two gentlemen in regal clothes, one being the prince, the other the Duke.

"Daughters?" the Duke asked.

"This way," she replied.

Cinderella saw the prince and bawled. Meanwhile, Drizella eagerly tried on the glass slipper, but her clown foot didn't fit. Anastasia slipped her foot into the small fragile glass slipper. To her surprise, her dainty little foot fit. She was astonished.

"We've found your bride!" the Duke said.

"We shall be betrothed tomorrow!" the prince announced.

Cinderella cried and cried.

Dhaani Pandya (11)

Langley Park School For Girls, Beckenham

UNSEEN WITNESS

A threatening smog gradually engulfed the avenue. *Tick-tock*. The pungent smell of soot and liquor permeated my nostrils. The Night-Man was here. Through my clouded vision, I could distinguish a gentleman meandering across the alley. *Tick-tock*. A brief whistle sounded. I held my breath. *Tick-tock*. The man's steps turned frantic. *Tick-tock*. A match was lit. *Tick-tock*. A gasp of air. A strangled cry. *Tick-tock*. A thud. Silence. Long, harrowing silence.
The streets alongside the alley buzzed. Yet nobody ventured inside. Nobody would dare face the Night-Man.
I chuckled as I lit another match. Nobody would dare face me...

Laura Sullivan (14)
Langley Park School For Girls, Beckenham

CHANGING TIMES

King Macbeth was protected in his palace. Or so he thought. His bodyguard ran into Macbeth's room yelling, "The woods are moving!"

However, Macbeth didn't believe him and shouted, "Liar!" and continued to look at CCTV and was shocked at the sight of camouflaged jeeps moving towards his palace. Macbeth pulled on his bulletproof vest, loaded his pistol and ran to meet them with his bodyguards, surrounding them.

At the end, Macduff's gang members were dead. So were Macbeth's bodyguards. Only they were left. Macduff raised his pistol and *boom!* Macbeth fell and a crowd gathered. "All hail, King Macduff!"

Isabella Travers (14)

Langley Park School For Girls, Beckenham

THE VILLAIN'S VIEW

I'm always seen as the villain, nobody cares about us. They only want us dead.

"Switchblade! I'm here to stop you!"

It gets boring fast. "Get on with it."

"You should be ashamed!"

"Oh, please! Heroes are selfish. They only care about money and fame. I should know. You left me to die as a child."

He stepped on the panel, oblivious to his fate. "Why is this warm?"

I smiled. "A rational person would spare you and move on. But luckily for me, I'm not a rational person." I watched as he crumbled into ashes. "Because I'm the villain."

Amélie Holst (14)

Langley Park School For Girls, Beckenham

BLOOD-SOAKED THRONES

"None shall live, all shall die. Come nightfall, all shall hail Macbeth." The whispered words lit a lust for blood in a hopeful man's eyes. An ambition none could smother.

As the sun rose the next morning the prophecy was completed. An unworthy man sat on a blood-soaked throne. Yet behind every throne lies a pair of lips. Whispered words behind darkened doors, urging looks from deceitful eyes, manipulative parents, sisters, wives. Each monarch has their own story, each more blood-soaked than the last.

The returning morning a new queen reigned, with her husband's blood soaking her hands.

Anna Greenwood (14)

Langley Park School For Girls, Beckenham

ROUND TWO

I watched through the window as my plan was unravelling. The seven dwarves were all surrounding her, saying their goodbyes. They all looked so sad and pathetic, which is what you get for helping such an ugly duckling.

But what's this? It's the prince. I must go introduce myself. "Your Majesty, I saw you from over there and I had to say hello." I did a curtsy and gave my hand out.

"Good evening, I must say you're very beautiful."

Twenty-five years later, I put a spell on the apple, getting déjà vu. "Round two, I am the most beautiful."

Mia Forrest (14)

Langley Park School For Girls, Beckenham

128

BEAMED

I'd been awake for a bit now. I was talking to this doctor, I think his name was McCoy and he sounded like he was from Texas, which is fun. And now this guy just came in. "Hello..." "Hi." I don't think he was expecting me to be awake. I overheard him talking to McCoy. I think his name was Spock. I told him so.

"Logical. You were the last to regain consciousness."

The last? I was confused. "The last?"

The door slid open and my best friends were there. I smiled. "Of course it's you."

"Erm, that's so rude."

Daisy Wallace (14)

Langley Park School For Girls, Beckenham

NANSEL AND BRETEL

Whilst stuck in the woods, Nansel and Bretel came across a mysterious house. They entered and discovered lots of food and expensive jewellery. They gathered as much as they could and filled their pockets.

They came across a kitchen and as they inspected it closer they noticed an oven turned on. As they neared the oven they cried out as Nansel and Bretel realised what they thought was dinner cooking was actually a middle-aged woman. The smell became unbearable. They covered their noses and mouths and ran out.

They ran all the way home. They're both now suspects.

Yasmine Amrane (14)
Langley Park School For Girls, Beckenham

LITTLE RED DARING HOOD

One summer's day in 1842, there was a grandmother and her grandchild who were highly respected in their community. One day, Grandmother was baking the finest bread and was writing a list of shopping for Little Red to buy for her.

As Little Red rushed out to buy them, an orange beam of light corroded the sky and sudden thuds bounced around the town. A huge shadow towered down. Little Red picked up her basket and charged speedily towards the wicked titan and started hitting the paws of the beast. Shortly after, the beast clasped onto her small body... *snap!*

Megan Ofori-Appiah (12)

Langley Park School For Girls, Beckenham

DEATH'S LAMENT

My work is long and hard each day. I am indifferent to death, for I am Death. That doesn't mean I wish for your demise, but I have learnt to turn a blind eye to the tragedies of humanity.

Every year I guide children to the other side from the Hunger Games. Today I bring another young girl home because of it. "Rue, we must leave," I say.

"I know, but..." She then points towards someone crying over her. "I want to be with Katniss a bit longer."

Although I am Death, I cannot say no to the little girl.

Emma Wallace (14)
Langley Park School For Girls, Beckenham

BEHIND THE BLINDS

I look to my right; the dark and mysterious but beautiful building stands in my presence. My curiosity tickles me and signals me to walk towards it. I peer through the window to see the most horrific sight. My whole body trembles and I start to sweat. He pushes the knife into the innocent soul and I stand there as white as snow.

I run back to my home but bump into someone unknowingly. They ask, "What's wrong?"

I explain what happened and their six-word answer strikes me. "That building was demolished in 1976."

Zahra Haman (11)

Langley Park School For Girls, Beckenham

ALADDIN AND ABU

My life was an adventure with my partner in crime! Stealing, running, hiding, until that all stopped. Our lives changed. From living in a hideout with no food to living in a mansion with unlimited food. He turned into the king and then forgot about me. We became strangers. He never spoke to me. He had other priorities now.

I left the palace heartbroken. I went back to my old ways, but it wasn't the same. I could never leave him completely. I watched his children grow up. As my life became worse, his became better. I really miss him.

Kitty-Mae Brown (14)
Langley Park School For Girls, Beckenham

OFF WITH HIS HEAD

I never wanted to be the queen. The thought of all that power would drive me insane, and it did. Just like everybody else in Wonderland, I went mad!

Sitting on my golden throne that was draped in crimson roses, I watched as the guards dragged in my next victim. There was no point listening to his pleading but he began to beg. It gave me a splitting headache and I was having a bad day so I screamed, "Off with his head!"

Blood splattered everywhere. I didn't feel bad because he had committed a crime. He deserved it!

Emma Wilson (14)

Langley Park School For Girls, Beckenham

THE VILLAIN'S VIEW

Why am I the villain? When Little Red Riding Hood came to me, I was only trying to save her. Why will nobody understand?

It all started when an old lady's cottage had a fire. When I saw a girl skipping through the forest I had to stop her from going in the cottage. Frantically, I tried to get her away but she wouldn't believe me.

Desperately, I sneaked into the cottage before she got there and wore her grandmother's clothes despite my razor-sharp teeth. I had no choice but to do this - I urgently had to save her.

Isla Wilton (12)
Langley Park School For Girls, Beckenham

A VOICE FOR THE VOICELESS

Trapped. Voiceless. My life is just waiting for the moment they murder me. Injecting me with poison. Who could be that cruel? I have to suffer in this world because of humans. They let me and all the other animals die. Torturing me, harassing me, they let me die slowly just so they can get new shampoo.

Gradually, I am getting weaker and weaker. Trapped, any moment could be my last breath. Why would you have a pet if you let me die? I'm surrounded by rattling cages, begging to be free. Death is upon us because of you.

Demi-Mae Woolcott (14)

Langley Park School For Girls, Beckenham

FROZEN: AN ALTERNATE REALITY

Today was the day. I was going to kill Elsa. She was using her powers so recklessly. I needed her power. I made a plan to suffocate her in her sleep. It was an easy plan.

I got my pillow and sneaked into her room. I straddled her and began to choke her. I felt her struggle and try to get me off, but it didn't work. My body filled with rage and then it was silent. I was satisfied.

I then heard heavy footsteps. "Anna, what're you doing?"

I was shocked. To my surprise, I was looking at Elsa.

Chesney Paul (14)
Langley Park School For Girls, Beckenham

I AM COBRA KAI

Nobody knows the truth. I have a weakness. Johnny Lawrence, my star student, All Valley champion. He had much potential and I ruined it for him. Made it about Cobra Kai.

Silver is dead meat. He thinks he can take over my dojo and falsely accuse me of assaulting someone. That sick snake. When I get my hands on him, he's dead. How dare he have the audacity to sabotage me and my students? Everyone sees me as the villain, but Silver is much worse in comparison. Truth be told, Silver is dead, and I am Cobra Kai.

Sahar Attaran (14)
Langley Park School For Girls, Beckenham

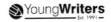

THE SUIT

I cannot believe him! He is so bad at his job. I don't understand why everyone loves him so much.

It's a Saturday night and he has just seen that there was a robbery in Times Square, New York, and he decided that it was a good idea to go and try to save the people there. When he got there, it was all fake news. Such a loser.

"I hate you Spider-Man, so much!"

"Wait, woah! You can speak?" said the loser.

"Ugh, yeah. I'm not just a normal suit!"

Alicia Boscornea (14)

Langley Park School For Girls, Beckenham

ALONE

I sit in the dark corner, slowly fading away. Dust collects in my hair and delicate cobwebs form above my head. I haven't heard her voice in so many long years. The warm sunlight seeps through the gap in the pink, floral curtains. The room is practically empty ever since she packed her bags and moved away. I miss the way she used to hug me when she cried and the way she used to dress me up in uncomfortable clothes. In my next life, I wish I could go with her. I wish I wasn't just a teddy bear.

Evie Kench (14)
Langley Park School For Girls, Beckenham

NO BRICKS JUST LUNCH

I had been watching them for ages, struggling with sticks and straw, such lazy little piggies. Every time they built a house, I huffed and I puffed and I blew the houses down. Watching their failure made me happy.

However, I saw bricks. One of them grabbed them and he started building. More and more bricks. My eyes widened and I knew I needed to do something. So I stole. I stole the rest of the bricks but it failed. So I ate. I ate them all up. I succeeded. I took my mask off to let out a snort.

Sinem Özbay (14)

Langley Park School For Girls, Beckenham

PART OF THEIR WORLD

I suddenly found myself surrounded by strangers. I was 15 when it happened. I still remember everything like it was yesterday. Truth be told, that was two years ago. I used to think of it as inescapable fate, death, never expecting it to be like this. My life ended two years ago but a new one began in a different world. Life here is better than all the fantasies as a kid. At first, I hated visiting my family in their world but now I realise this is where I belong. This was always going to be my home.

Eloise Dewey (13)
Langley Park School For Girls, Beckenham

BAT TO BACK

My blood boiled when I saw him holding a baseball bat. *Bang!* He thumped me before I could react. Everything was complete darkness.

I picked up the latest newspaper and the date read 2002. No way, it couldn't be. I must be in a dream. I pinched myself and realised this was real.

I sprinted to the closest toilet to check this was definitely real. I looked in the mirror and all of my wrinkles were gone. My hair wasn't going grey anymore and my face looked so much younger.

Anna Gladwell (14)
Langley Park School For Girls, Beckenham

WHO THE QUEEN WAS

When I was eighteen years old, I became queen. It wasn't my fault, I didn't want it - I had to. When I was a child I had a name, not a title. I was Cygnus and I was a prisoner. My mother tutored me in potions and weapons, and how to be a queen, like it was always meant to be. I never wanted any of it, but if I didn't obey I was punished.

Now, a grown adult with a kingdom and a title, I still obey and fear her. I am not Cygnus anymore, I'm the Evil Queen.

Emily Read (13)

Langley Park School For Girls, Beckenham

ONE DIFFERENCE

Bored. Bored. Bored. I've been stuck in the same old room since it ended. Since he won. Now everyone who doesn't fit his standards is in danger. No one is safe in his reign. Hitler's reign. All I can do is stay put and hope for the best. Just then the door is broken and he blocks the way. That tyrant. Hitler.

Kayla Shirley (15)
Langley Park School For Girls, Beckenham

THE JOKER'S BACKSTORY

Nobody knows the truth about me, why I'm a villain. I'm not evil just misunderstood. Before I was a villain, before anything, I was once loved by people. I was the butt of all jokes in the town.

But one day my mom fell ill with cancer. I needed money for her treatment, but I had no money. I had no choice but to go to the life of crime.

After I had the money it was already over. I was ignored and unloved. But the only way to be noticed was to become a villain.

Mohammad Ali (11)
Lynch Hill Enterprise Academy, Slough

THE BOY WHO DIED

The glass from the window splashed everywhere, gliding past his dad, spitting blood out from his cheek. A dark presence could be sensed coming from the window. First, a leg came over, then the second. It was Voldermort. A green splutter like lightning shot out, coming from his wand and his dad folded to the floor. His mum quickly shot to the door, obscuring his vision from inside the cot. The door splintered, knocking her down. She was killed in front of him. Voldemort shouted, "Avada Kedavra!" Green came out. Harry had no scar. He was the boy who died.

Leo Brazier (14)
Magdalen College School, Oxford

BREAKING POINT

Winnie the Pooh sat propped up against a tree, just at the edge of Christopher Robin's garden. It was raining heavily. This was the third this had happened this week and he'd had enough. He looked around and saw his target's window and plodded towards the house, picking up the baseball bat along the way, dragging it along the floor. He scaled the drainpipe and got to Christopher Robin's window. He looked in and saw him sleeping there so soundly. The red mist came over his eyes as he prepared to enact his vengeance on his old 'friend'...

Edward Rugman (14)
Magdalen College School, Oxford

JUST A STORMTROOPER

TK 411: That was what they used to call me. Just another drone in white-painted armour. I was an old Stormtrooper - one of the originals. Washed up, worn out and still just an unimportant white, walking carcass - only good for battle and sacrifice, nothing else. By now that murderous red flash that escaped my rifle every time the trigger was pulled was so recognisable to me. I could name every deepened shade inside without having to look. I had killed so many and for what? A moment of alleged peace? Well, at least I would be dead soon.

Edward Craven (13)
Millthorpe School, York

MY NIGHTMARE MIGHT HAVE BECOME TRUE

"Logan, breakfast is ready."

I get up, put my dressing gown on and go downstairs. Yes! Pancakes, my favourite. I put some on my plate and sit at the dinner table.

"I'm popping out to the shop," Mum says.

I finish my pancakes and put my plate in the sink. I've been wanting to find this football forever so while Mum is out I decide I'm going to find it so now she can't tell me off for going through stuff. I walk into this little room, bodies, blood.

I wake up. I hear my mum. "Logan, breakfast is ready..."

Sandra Gawranowska (12)
Minsthorpe Community College, South Elmsall

SORRY NAT, SORRY SISTER

Everybody trusts their sister, right? We all know they can be a pain sometimes yet they wouldn't kill you would they? I thought that once as well. September 1st 1987... Back then my sister and I were escaping a school shooting. We hid everywhere we could to survive. I had protected her more than I protected myself. The tragedy caused many issues in our family last night. I believe we all deserve a second chance. What else could I have done when the murderous monster walked in? I grabbed the knife from my bag and killed my sister dead.

Maisie Mccann (12)
Minsthorpe Community College, South Elmsall

THE DEATH OF LITTLE RED RIDING HOOD

It was a bright day, the sun was shining. Trees were swaying in the breeze. Birds were twittering. I was feeling very hungry. In the forest it was damp. Leaves crunched against my paws. I went searching for food. There was nothing but sticks, leaves, mud and grass. Everything was blowing in the wind. I spotted a lonely girl tumbling through the forest. She was as small as a rat. Clattering came from the bottom of her bright pink shoes. I decided to follow her. I was too hungry. I crept up behind her and gobbled her up in one.

Ella Iveson (12)
Minsthorpe Community College, South Elmsall

THE TRUTH WAS LEFT BEHIND

Hues of orange and yellow ink carpeted the blue parchment of the sky. This was my happy place.

With that, my crystalline glass heart shattered. Thousands of its fragments blanketed the floor. And though each displayed kaleidoscope reflections, my world was slowly becoming darker. The array of colours soon drifted into the horizon, making way for the moon to begin its reign. The moon hovered above like a ghostly galleon, a sea of clouds attempting to drown it.

This was such a perfect life. Except nothing was real. It was all just an illusion. The truth was left behind.

Mia Simpkin (12)
Montgomery Academy, Blackpool

WHO IS THE KILLER?

Twenty-three. Twenty-three people have been killed in the past week. Doors were locked, windows too. Not a sound could be heard across this cursed town. Until I heard a window smash.

My eyes darted to my bedroom door, heart knocking at my chest. My first instinct was to hide, so I did. Like a real-life horror film, I had never been so scared, hiding behind my wardrobe. My breath shuddered.

My name outside my door. A familiar voice. Hesitant, I opened the door. I couldn't believe my eyes. My best friend stood before me, breathless and covered in blood.

Sophie-Louise Hadfield (13)
Montgomery Academy, Blackpool

CURSED LIPS

It was too late, she was gone. "Sleeping with the fishes," as her mother so lovingly put it. The prince had kissed her in a desperate attempt to save his 'damsel in distress'. He stood for a moment, lips parted, eyes wide. He stared down at Snow as his face turned red and hands grasped his throat as if he couldn't speak. The prince fell to the floor, beside the glass coffin, the dwarves gathered around him, all sharing equal worry.

But there was someone else, behind the trees. A tall, dark figure with a malicious smile. The evil queen.

Tillie Thompson (13)
Montgomery Academy, Blackpool

COME BACK

We were at the library all day. We found the book we were looking for - 'A Guide To Making Things You Probably Shouldn't Make'. I chuckled at the name, it's comedic after all.

We walked to my house. I found myself staring at her face over the time we spent together. We worked tirelessly.

I entered the living room after our twelve days of labour. I looked at what we'd done. We'd made a working portal to her world of humans. She went through the portal. It closed. I never told her that I love her. I want her back...

Lei Austin (13)
Montgomery Academy, Blackpool

A CENTAUR MYTH

In a small humble town, a myth rose about a centaur. People said he was a cold-blooded murderer but that isn't the real truth.

It all started at the very beginning. Some people were in the forest. They shouted monster at the centaur and people thought the centaur killed them after. But in reality, nature killed them. People thought he shot a boulder but a cliff just broke and someone fell. But the others didn't see and got to the village.

The centaur thought people would hate him and hid. Little did he know, they knew the truth.

Sam Lu (13)
Montgomery Academy, Blackpool

SHHH... HE'S WATCHING YOU

I woke up. *Where am I? Why am I here?* I opened my eyes and let my eyes adjust to the darkness. I wasn't alone. Someone else was here with me.

I went to wake him up and after a while, he woke up. He then explained to me that we were trapped here and every week a person came in and killed someone in the room, and that I would never escape and that it wasn't worth the trouble.

I didn't listen. I should have; maybe, just maybe it would've saved my life. The murderer looked up at me.

Anni Yu (12)
Montgomery Academy, Blackpool

THE FROZEN HAND

I suddenly found myself in a pitch-black, mysterious cave. I looked around and I saw a shadow of what I can only assume was a person, dressed in a cloak, slowly walking towards me. But then they just disappeared.

It was too dark to recognise the person. But something about them seemed familiar. I started to feel around to try and find a way out of the mystifying cave. But then an icy hand slowly rested on my shoulder and I froze!

Then I started sprinting away from the frozen hand and then I tripped on a sharp rock...

Blake Bills (15)
North Herts ESC, Hitchin

DEATH

Death is beautiful and kind. People usually don't say that about me. Everybody sees me as a monster who takes away your loved ones. Brings them to a fate they didn't want. Gives them pain. Gives you grief. But my job is simply to escort souls to Hell or Heaven. I help them transition. Some people don't want to go, I've had plenty of times when I'd had to convince somebody to walk with me. So, when people say I'm the bad guy, I scoff. Because when the end comes, I'll bring you to the people who you've loved most.

Lily Moden (15)
Northease Manor School, Newhaven

SEA FOAM

(Inspired by 'The Little Mermaid' by Hans Christian Andersen)

He could have had anyone he wanted, but he wanted her. She was always top of the world, platinum, gold, awards. He was from a different corner of the world. He wanted to be part of hers. He wanted to walk with the elite. Instead, she found somebody else. A realtor or a lawyer or some con artist from a shopping channel. They fit together perfectly in Hollywood, as he was left as drunken seafoam at the bottom of his pool.

Johnny Angel (15)
Northease Manor School, Newhaven

THE ROOM OF LIFE AND DEATH

I'm waiting for our guest to arrive at our room. Finally, the young man arrives and talks to the man who I assist here, He says the same thing as always, "Welcome, this is a room placed between dreams and reality." The young man decides his demons to combine. I go and get the guillotine ready as always. My master places the demons into the guillotine, I let the rope go and the merciless blade rapidly descends without a thought and they scream for a second, but then magically fuse. The young man leaves and I wait again in silence.

Aidan Shephard Garcia (15)

Padworth College, Padworth

THE ONE RING MAKES ITS CHOICE

Today is the day. I am never going to serve under Sauron again. I've witnessed too much death caused by him. It was torture. I will never go back. I understand what needs to be done. I have to die. But, in order to make this journey I will be forced to help Frodo fight the evil that will try to corrupt his heart just like I'd done with Bilbo. Only this time it's going to be much more challenging, as we will have to face a much greater evil. It's been decided I'm going to help the brave Hobbit.

Alainor Sefton (15)
Padworth College, Padworth

THE STARVING FILLIP

Once upon a time, there was a caterpillar called Fillip. Fillip was an extremely hungry caterpillar who could never stop eating. Fillip's eating habit was so bad that the local area ran out of food but Fillip was just too hungry and was looking for food from far, far away. Eventually, Fillip got lost and couldn't find his way home. He said to himself, "It's fine, I can make a new home here up in the trees." He made his new home not too high up in the trees. After he woke up he died from over-eating food.

Kaiden Parker (12)

Parkside Academy, Willington

VOLDEMORT'S SIDE

That good wizardry act was fake, they stole my family, and tried to kill me. All because my family knows the ultimate power. Dumbledore figured out and he locked my family in magic-taking chambers in Hogwarts. He's convinced lots of people that I'm the evil one to cover up this terrible, dark secret. I'm just trying to save my loving family, I miss them. I will do anything in my power to stop him and enlighten everyone about his dark lie. Even if that means stopping Harry and his friends from trying to defeat me. *I will enlighten them.*

Caiden Maskell (12)
Penrice Academy, St Austell

THE WOLF CHASE

We all know the story about the little boy who lied about seeing a big, bad, petrifying wolf. But did he lie? Little did this prankster know, he was staring into his own reflection from a distanced river that the sun was beaming off. *Boom!* It hit him. He wasn't lying. *He* was the big, bad wolf all along. "Arghhh!" The boy heard a few screams and screeches. He saw a crowd of people running but didn't think anything of it. He raised his head slowly to see a herd of wolves chasing after him. He tried to run! RIP.

Ava Plimley (14)
Pensby High School, Heswall

LITTLE RED

The plan was in motion. Red Riding Hood placed her cheek on the fidgety handle of the shotgun and aimed down the scope. She waited hours and hours. No sight of the monstrosity of a monster they call the wolf until in the silence of the night, Red Riding Hood heard leaves crumbling in the distance. She saw a wrinkled beast covered in thick grey hair. Without hesitation, she fired the shot. *Bang!* Its head came clean off, landing at Red Riding Hood's feet. But as the debris cleared, she saw the head of her grandma lying in the dust.

Dylan Hughes (14)
Pensby High School, Heswall

RAPUNZEL

It was a normal day until Rapunzel wasn't acting herself, every time I went near her she pushed me away. Seconds later, I heard Flynn shout, "Rapunzel, let down your hair." She went over, he was climbing up until Rapunzel grabbed a knife and cut her hair. Flynn fell straight down, bleeding everywhere. He was dead. Rapunzel turned around and saw her mother standing there, giving her an evil look. She grabbed the knife out of Rapunzel's hand and stabbed her in her tummy. I was in shock. I didn't know what I was going to do...

Emily Strachan (13)
Plympton Academy, Plympton

THE STEPMOTHER'S TRUTH

Nobody knew the truth about me. My husband died last year on my birthday which left me heartbroken. Since then, I haven't been myself.

I've cared for my children a lot more since and wanted to do the same for Cinderella, but my broken heart took over. All my life with Cinderella I tried my hardest; it didn't last long. I loved Cinderella deep down, I swear. I just couldn't show it. I wish I'd changed before and now Cinderella has left. I made a huge mistake. I never tried at all. I couldn't. I wish I could restart everything.

Aisha Yafai (12)
Queen Mary's High School, Walsall

MISSING POTTER

Nobody knew what happened to me, it's been months. Ever since that day, I found the invisible cloak I've been lonely and hopeless. I was screaming and crying in alleyways just hoping someone would hear me. I just wish I could go back to the old me. Then I had an idea, maybe the box the cloak came in had a cure! I opened it up and there was a blue glowing light. It was blinding but I searched for anything to help. Then I saw devilish spirits fly out. "Oh no! What did I do? Help me!"

Resham Lakhanpal (13)
Regents Park Community College, Regents Park

PEPPA PIG'S TEMPER TANTRUM

Pots fell off the bench, flowers smashed, couches ripped, TV thrown and George dead! Peppa's parents cowered in fear down in the basement waiting for pet control to arrive as Peppa ravaged and destroyed everything in her path. It felt like hours waiting for pet control as Peppa ransacked the house from head to toe. *Knock, knock, knock!* They were here! As Mummy Pig and Daddy Pig stumbled up the stairs pet control was already on the task. Giant nets and stun guns to keep her at bay as they escorted her out ready for the butcher.

Mariam Noori (12)
Rockwood Academy, Birmingham

THE ACCIDENT

It was a normal day and Lucy was walking her dog across the road but then Tim, her dog got hit by a bus. Lucy was so close to Tim that she punched the car window and threatened the driver. The police arrived and took Lucy away to prison. She was sentenced to six months for the death threat. In prison, she fell into depression as she didn't get to go to Tim's funeral. She cried to see Tim once again. On the day she got out of prison she stepped outside and with a very shocked expression saw Tim...

Mahek Rehman (11)
Rockwood Academy, Birmingham

GUY FAWKES

The silence was disturbed. Catastrophe struck. My plan was left undiscovered until now. I succeeded in the blowing up of parliament; my lifelong goal. For years, I had been devising this plan. The plan that ruined society. The plan that made not me, but my work, infamous. How had I gotten away with this? My humour ignites when the memories of that night come rushing back to me. The incessant screams of fear fill my brain each night, along with the rumble of the building collapsing. What was a dreadful night for history, became a triumphant night for me.

Rosie Wilkins (14)
Sir Robert Pattinson Academy, North Hykeham

CURED

The plan was going smoothly, or so the piglets thought. As soon as Mr Wolf climbed the chimney, he saw it: the boiling pot of water. He imagined the pigs sniggering while eating him for dinner; he wasn't going to let that happen. He placed his large, furry, rounded bottom on top of the chimney. Smoke started filling the room below. The pigs began frantically coughing. Later that evening, Mrs Wolf asked, "What's for dinner, my dear?"
"Smoked bacon," chuckled her husband.

Tom Lewis (11)
Solefield School, Sevenoaks

BLINDED BY LOVE

You call out my name every day. You go on - incessantly - about how much you want to set me free from this tower. Fool! I want to be here. I want to be alone. You never listen to me, so I will never listen to you. Your words are meaningless now, empty as air.

There was one part of me that loved you, but that's gone. When I was young and vain, throwing down my golden locks was such a joy. Older and wiser, I despise it. That's why you will never be seeing me again... (or anyone else...)

Barnaby Tym (11)
Solefield School, Sevenoaks

THE FORESHADOWING

I was 5 when I first saw the future. Now the war is raging in Germany. I have seen that we will win the war, but I haven't told anyone. Tom has been begging to join the army, but Father and Edgar are very against it. Tom is only 14. However, Mother is very willing to let him risk his young life. Edgar has been given multiple white feathers because he hasn't gone to war and he is 20. Tom has left without saying goodbye. My premonition can't fail me now...

Aidan Clarke (12)
Southend High School For Boys, Westcliff-On-Sea

THE HIDDEN TRUTH

He suddenly found himself in an abnormal situation. His own family was murdered by his three older brothers. The four ninja turtles were no more. Michaelangelo had only one reason to live, to kill his own brothers. He grew up to be a fine ninja turtle. The time had come when he would fight his brothers. He killed them with his own power. But, just before they died, they told him the truth. The leader of Mountain Myoboku forced them to murder their family, their clan. Michaelangelo believed them but his hatred made him kill them. Michaelangelo knew they lied.

Gjulio Gjoka
Southfields Academy, Wandsworth

KAI'S 100-WORD MYSTERY

I still haven't forgotten the time when I was a child. Me and my mate were riding through the woods on quads and we saw a house made out of Nike shoes. We stopped but this was a big mistake. We slowly walked to the house and admired the new red Jordan special edition trainers. Then suddenly, out of nowhere, an old man jumped out at us. He grabbed us but we got free and ran to the quads. Later that night, we went back with nine-inch weapons, killed the guy, took the shoes and quickly rode off.

Kai Howell (12)

St Andrew's CE High School, Worthing

THE GIRL IN THE MANSION

Bones crackling, the sound of blood travelling slowly down her frock, faded breathing in and out. There she lay as the thunder roared, rain pattering like children's footsteps, a reminder of what once was. The knife that purged her and the heart that bled. The mansion became cold and bitter. A smell of death lingered in the once-alive home. The butler made to serve, who the girl had trusted her entire life, there she lay in his arms, for he was the one to go for the kill. He was the one who took her life against her will.

Jade Fleet (15)
St Augustine Academy, Maidstone

FLOUNDER'S POINT OF VIEW

She came to meet me at the water's edge every day after she got her legs. She would say how much walking hurt, saying it felt like she was walking on swords daily. I knew she couldn't take it but she wouldn't give up on Prince Eric. Ariel was desperate for him. I couldn't believe my eyes when one day she came to me crying, her eyes bloodshot. I knew for a fact that something was wrong. Then I realised. It'd been three days and the prince hadn't fallen in love with her. But there was nothing I could do.

Sophie Cosnett (12)
St Barnabas CE First & Middle School, Drakes Broughton

JACK, JILL AND A MONSTROSITY

Jack ran as fast as ever, his heart thumping in his chest. He saw Jill go up the hill, assumed he would catch up, but when he did all he saw was a tarnished body while a wendigo ate at her remains after crawling out of the well. The icy hands of dread caressed his heart with serrated fingers, and he let out a scream. The wendigo looked up from its meal and gave chase, launching itself at Jack. What could Jack do to avoid this monstrosity? It seemed impossible but slowly, half an idea formed in his fearful heart...

Ashton Cox (12)
St Barnabas CE First & Middle School, Drakes Broughton

THE TRUE STORY OF JAWS

The poachers were hunting me. I had nowhere else to go. I'm sorry. Once upon a time, I was forced into a shallow beach. There was nothing I could do and there was nothing to feed on. So there I was, stranded with no cover and no food. Except people. I didn't want to do it, but I had to. The innocent people of that island were my only hope of survival. And now there are stories of a dreadful shark terrorising people for no reason. I wish they knew. Then I would be safe from them. All of them.

Barnaby Boucker (12)

St Barnabas CE First & Middle School, Drakes Broughton

HANSEL AND GRETEL

The witch was getting the sweet cottage perfect, adding the last touches to her adorable trap of death. She had predicted that she would have some small visitors before the day's end. She waited and waited until they came searching. She invited them in, planning her gruesome plan. She was reminded about her husband, who got killed by a rage of orphan children back when they were treated like savages. Just as she was getting revenge, someone tapped on her back. Out of curiosity, she turned around, finding the small one behind her! She was never seen after that day.

Annie Fichardt (12)
St Catherine's School, Bramley

SPEECHLESS

I used to say too much and now I can't say anything at all. Here's my story.

I was gazing out at a gorgeous starry night. I'd looked away for barely a second and when I looked back I saw a boy with hair a peculiar shade of red that could only be compared to Mars and his eyes brown like the dirt on his face. He lured me out of my bedroom and flew me to Neverland. Then he put his hand on me and the last thing I remembered as I fell was not being able to scream.

Charlotte Ebsworth (13)
St Catherine's School, Bramley

OUR WORLD

I have to tell you, telling this story makes my stomach turn upside down like a roller coaster with loops, as if it's happening all over again. Day fifteen, fifteen days ago a tragic event occurred. Our thin layer of time itself broke, sending our world into a week of despair and misery. Medieval clans roaming since 1700 came back into our reality to take back what once was theirs. A frantic free-for-all broke out, killing anyone who stood in their way. They made their way to a field and had a standoff. But I woke up...

Samuel Clare (12)
Sybil Andrews Academy, Bury St Edmunds

HELA

For years I'd dreamed of the moment I would destroy him. Finally the day had come. My father banished me from this castle whilst my petite brothers had all they could desire. I burst through the doors and began to stride through the corridor that I once owned. I realised he got rid of my picture, well now I would destroy more than just his painting, I was here to kill Odin. I could see him as clear as glass. I approached, ready to kill. Then I saw my mother. I realised I could not do this. I took off.

Lucas Palframan (12)
Sybil Andrews Academy, Bury St Edmunds

THE HEIST

Today was the big day, the competition was closing and the results would be posted. I'd been waiting for two weeks. My mum was ill so I needed the money. The results said I came... third. I needed to get £2,651 more so I could afford her surgery. I felt like I needed to rob a ship or find a way to get a lot of money...

On the ship there were pirates and two were guarding the treasure, so I snuck past, took it and rowed in a small raft. I paid the hospital and she got the surgery.

Joshua Campbell-Hissett (11)

Sybil Andrews Academy, Bury St Edmunds

CREATURE

It was a normal day for Quandale and he went to his locker and heard a loud banging. He saw the top row of lockers dented and his was open. He looked in his locker. There were sizzling holes going through the panels. Something had been here. Something different. He had a shot of fear fly through him. Then a rustling in the bin a metre away from him. Then he heard a gargle. He did not know what to do. He walked over to the bin, he took a look...

Coby Alton (12)
Sybil Andrews Academy, Bury St Edmunds

THE FUNERAL SURPRISE

Once upon a time there were three boys, Travis, Lewis and Riley. They were cruising in a Lamborghini. When Riley was in the car he got shot and then they all went to Riley's funeral. Then he woke up and everyone was really shocked because they didn't know this would happen. Then they all left and made a treehouse in a tree and had a disco. It was all really fun.

Travis Hope (11)
Sybil Andrews Academy, Bury St Edmunds

CINDERELLA, ANOTHER VERSION

Their horrible stepsister takes their phones and smashes them against the wall and instantly blames the damage on Linda and Heather. Cinderella gets away with it. Cinderella is horrible and jealous of Linda and Heather, in fact as soon as Linda and Heather get invitations to the ball she steals them before they can get their hands on them and goes to the ball instead.

Daisy Sturdey (12)
Tarporley High School, Tarporley

ROBIN HOOD OF NOTTINGHAM

I have to tell you... I have discovered Robin Hood's secret! I have seen an important letter from the Sheriff of Nottingham. Robin is not a good guy. The important news is that Robin has been robbing! He does take from the rich but he doesn't give it all to the poor. I am going to kidnap him, chop off his finger and expose him to the whole of Nottingham. When Nottingham finds out, they will be terrified of Robin Hood. And so they should be! He will not stop robbing the rich and the poor people. They will die!

Adam Butt (13)
Teenage Kicks, Failsworth

THE SLEEPING TRUTH

Nobody knew the truth about me... The queen and I were best friends. Travelling, secrets, films. She ruined my life. I was heartbroken with nobody to talk to. The queen announced her marriage. I saw them on TV. Her and the love of my life. I was sinking into the ground. I made a plan to get revenge. I wanted her to be as upset as I was when they had her first child. She'd feel what it was like to lose something you cared so much about.
Sleeping Beauty was now 16. At last, I would get my revenge.

Fiona Collins (15)
Teenage Kicks, Failsworth

LIARS GET CAUGHT

It was a normal day until I saw Emily acting differently. She had her hood over her head and was looking at the floor. So I followed her into the school trying to catch up with her to scare her and warn her someone was after her, but it was too late. She ran into a classroom and this other person followed her and tried to kill her. Looking for Ezra to check and mark her work, she came across the other person in all dark clothes. She couldn't see their face or who it was. She had to run...

Skye Robinson (15)
Teenage Kicks, Failsworth

WHY ME?

It was just a normal day in maths class. Then a swirl of smoke surrounded me. A sickly feeling came over me and I closed my eyes then everything went quiet. I opened my eyes and I was in space... except I could breathe and I was on a floating island made of some sort of strange rock. In front of me was a strange purple tree with pink leaves and huge roots, with what looked like a house inside.
Someone walked in front of a window and looked at me. I fell back and was suddenly back in class.

Samuel Burke (13)
The Community College, Bishops Castle

SUPERNOVA

Nina's friends sat in a circle with hot chocolate and blankets. A speaker played music, quiet enough to hear discussions. The stars were out really bright. It was mid-August after all. She lay back on the grass taking in the view of the stars. Although the music and chatter drowned out, the vast night sky became clearer. Nina knew what would happen now. The brightest shooting star raced through the night, creating a large tail. In this star's tail she saw her future, although it was just a mixture of colours she could read the whole thing. She was stunned.

Isla Gardner (15)
The Open Academy, Norwich

REVENGE ON THE RIPPER

Oh hello. You really shouldn't be here. Do you know who I am? Guess not since I am a master at hiding my identity. I am Jack the Ripper. I'm not saying my real name in case you're a spy. You see that person there? That's Mary Jane Kelly. She will go down in history as one of the victims of the legendary Jack the Ripper. You might want to look away for this bit. Wait... Is that police? Hide around the corner, quick. They've never protected someone like this before. Run! Just run! I think I've finally been exposed.

James Hoye (15)
The Open Academy, Norwich

REGRETS

My dreams had come true, I had finally defeated my mortal enemy. But, I didn't feel any joy. I felt completely numb as the man I swore to one day kill lay dead in my arms. Where was the sense of victory and joy? All I felt was hollow. I didn't cry or laugh maniacally as my one life mission was accomplished. It was just silence as I looked down at him as the scarlet river seeped into his clothes. What do I do now? This was my life's purpose. I have no other goals. Was this a mistake?

Lisa Kracewicz (15)
The Open Academy, Norwich

THE ACT OF UNEON NEVER HAPPENED?

The day opens and the sun is shining over Edinburgh. My loyal servant rushes to me with a sealed letter from England. The letter states that George IV is recovering from his illness and that the plan of union when he does won't be needed. While reading that I was glad that I didn't have a personal union with England due to the religion of both nations. With a full day of working with parliament about new laws, the economy and diplomatic relations with other nations, I get back to my golden palace. As my eyes shut the day closes.

Daniel Mawby (13)
The Roseland Academy, Tregony

FOR OUR PROTECTION

After a string of violent terrorist attacks, killing thousands, dubbed 'The Red Summer' in 2036, Prime Minister, Lee Andrew, recognised that Great Britain needed a reform of its defence and security policy.

On December 2nd 2036, parliament passed the citizen protection and defence bill, allowing them access to all and any of its citizens' data. The police force was replaced with a militia who frequently patrolled the streets with their firearms. The amount of surveillance doubled, even surpassing China in 2039.

There were many who protested this change, many who were never seen again and many who still resist today.

Matas Konstantinov (14)

The Royal Liberty School, Gidea Park

BOMBAY

I'm in Bombay, India. I've rented an Indian elephant named Carnatic. She's helped me on my violent squalls and we're on a venture to success. The vast extent of our journey will bring everlasting impunity and security.

This time, instead of evil, I feel bipolar. Carnatic was rough and heavy, the heat of India was brandishing my sensitive skin and our route was at least eight weeks long. China's where we'll go but Carnatic is rebelling! A revolt! She is too tired to keep going! I'm deserted, stranded. Suddenly, I spit out paint. What's happening? Carnatic is gone. I'm deserted...

Revin Kazim (13)
The Royal Liberty School, Gidea Park

PLAN 44

The plan is in motion... He is nearly ready to die. I shall kill him. I must, to end their suffering. No one else will have to get hurt. One simple bullet to the head and it is all over. Millions of lives saved. And I, their unknown saviour. There he is. Surrounded. Bodyguards everywhere. No stone unturned. No extra blood spilt. No more lives taken. No more war... *Bang!* Bullet straight to the head. The body drops and rolls. One clean shot, straight through the head. No witnesses... *Bang! Bang! Bang!* They are all dead... Hitler is dead...

Aqeel Miah (14)
The Royal Liberty School, Gidea Park

YOU MAY NEVER FORGET

It was another normal day until me and my friends found this rotting door. Green liquid squelched out of it and the handle had started... melting? A sign 'you may never forget'. That was a few hours ago, we got sucked in like a vacuum. There we were, the six of us, just six children hiding in a dark alley. We were seven before but let's just say he had no brain but he definitely doesn't now...

There we were, the two of us, all alone. Crying... In another time an abnormal burnt letter arrived saying 'you may never forget'...

Ashleigh Wansi (14)
The Royal Liberty School, Gidea Park

THE FINAL ONE

I suddenly found myself in the future, after just waking up still feeling weary. There was nobody in town, even though it should've been packed. My first thought was, *where was everyone and is it just me here?* Without thinking about it, I turned on the TV. I was flabbergasted. The first channel was about a zombie apocalypse but I assumed it was a TV show. I scrolled through every channel and that was all it was about. Without notice, there was a sudden banging on my door. I panicked. My thought was, *it could be human.* It wasn't.

Bipin Acharya (13)
The Royal Liberty School, Gidea Park

RED SKY, BROKEN HEARTS

Day two of the outbreak. We've lost fifteen of our class. Helicopters keep flying past us. The field is red. The sky is red. I'm going to die soon. I just feel it. Death is in the air around me. We've cleared two floors using broken broomsticks and lousy kitchen knives. They just come back. It doesn't stop.

We had to climb down the building once because we lost too many in the music room. Now we're at the top. The roof is where someone can see us, maybe the army, I don't care. Just come and save us. Now.

Varun Teeluck (14)
The Royal Liberty School, Gidea Park

BETRAYAL

He lies on the floor, his blue sword seeping from its handle like his blood and life seeps from his body. I press my sharp nails up to his throat. He is ruined. I'm ruined. I look at myself and him. I am no human. Pieces of my bones are connected to pieces of machine. My skin is green with bloodshot scars across my arms. My helmet is nailed to my brain, ready to crush my skull if I betray my new master. "Please don't do this," he pleads.

"Goodbye, master," as I pull his throat from his neck.

Liam Kelly (14)
The Royal Liberty School, Gidea Park

THE TRUE STORY

No one knew... no one cared... I was once good... but they didn't believe me. I am Jack Calliger aka The Reaper. I was actually once a normal person, I had a wife and two kids. It was the perfect life. It all started when I headed off to work. The construction site was quite busy but it didn't stop me from working. I climbed into the crane and began working. All of a sudden, it started raining, so I quickly wanted to finish my last block but... it slipped. Twelve people dead, one survived. He ran, knowing my intention.

Azuolas Kersevicius (13)

The Royal Liberty School, Gidea Park

THE PORTAL

I woke up. The first thing I felt was my throbbing head. "Where am I?" I asked myself. My eyes started to open. This was not Earth! The sky was painted red along with the dead and decrepit trees. I was frozen from the fear that filled me. Then an inhuman growl echoed behind me. "What was that?" I got up and a gaunt, pale, nine-foot monster stood over me.

I ran for my life, trying to find a way out. Then I saw a portal. This was my only chance to live.

"I made it!" I survived...

Oliver Roberts (14)

The Royal Liberty School, Gidea Park

NOBODY KNEW

Nobody knew the truth about me. To everyone, I was just a normal guy in school. Nobody knew my secret. Every day I would go down to my secret bunker. I would plan my next attack. Each one had to be different to the ones before. If I created a pattern I would be caught. Every day, different place, different time, different clothes.

I don't know how I got to this point, but I was so used to doing it, it became second nature. It wouldn't be easy to stop. The most important part was that nobody knew the truth.

Aleksas Martinkus (14)
The Royal Liberty School, Gidea Park

THE WOLF WITH A COLD

It was a cold winter night when Mr Wolf had been kicked out of his home because he sneezed too much. He started off by going down to the pharmacy to get some medicine but on his way there he saw some in Mr Pig's window, so he went up and knocked on the door and asked. Mr Pig said, "No." He sneezed and blew down two of the pigs' houses. He tried to say I'm sorry but couldn't. The wolf explained so the pigs handed Mr Wolf some medicine and had a nice dinner. They lived happily ever after.

Christian Stanley (13)
The Royal Liberty School, Gidea Park

THE ATTACK

It was then that I noticed everyone was gone. It was pitch-black so I started going back home. I saw a little girl wearing a bright red outfit. She was walking down a small road and entered a small house at the end. I carried on walking the other way until I heard a scream. I looked through the window. Someone was attacking her. I jumped through the window and pounced on the person attacking her. I pulled her hat off and pushed them off the bed. I picked her up and threw her in the cupboard and locked it.

Teddy Wells (13)
The Royal Liberty School, Gidea Park

MY SON IS IMPORTANT

Nobody knew the truth about my son. I was on top of a hill with my son when he wanted to help the pigs. He had a cold that day. I saw him trying to move the bricks to help construct the house when he sneezed. The pigs sprinted away like headless chickens thinking that he would eat them. My son is vegan. He knocked on their door begging for forgiveness as he destroyed two of their homes. However, they shoved him into the oven! Now everyone in town dubbed him the big bad wolf even though he is innocent!

Lee Fisher (13)
The Royal Liberty School, Gidea Park

THE ESCAPE

I got back from work after a stressful day. I sat on the sofa. The doorbell rang. I answered it. It was the police. They showed me their badges and barged through the door. They said that I have to go somewhere. I scrambled into their car with a blindfold on. I ended up in a prison. As the metal gates opened, I saw my chance to run. I sprinted my way out of there and saw a staircase heading to the sky. I made my way to the top. Suddenly, I woke up and it was a hallucination.

Tommy Randall (13)
The Royal Liberty School, Gidea Park

AN ALTERNATIVE ENDING TO THE HARE AND THE TORTOISE

The mountain's fastest creature just couldn't be Hare, so I challenged him to a competition and he accepted. However, he wasn't aware that my twin brother would help me. We agreed that in the middle of the race he would emerge from his disguise and replace me. We followed our plan, but Hare was doubtful of our victory and he overheard us sharing the reward. Subsequently, the pesky carrot-eater reported us to Sheriff Snake and Jay Judge ordered us to be thrown off a cliff as punishment, so our shells would be damaged. So technically, Hare won the race.

Amelia Ali (12)
The Ursuline Academy Ilford, Ilford

UNEXPECTED CHANGE!

The darkest forest ever known, Red Riding Hood lived with her medieval mother who was only 49 years old. Mother asked her cherished daughter, Red Riding Hood, to go give her grandma some appetising cookies. Little Red Riding Hood skipped through the mechanism of the forest and as she skipped, she saw an unforeseen figure. It was a ferocious wolf and Red Riding Hood panicked as if she saw a dragon. She dashed until she saw her grandma's cottage up ahead. When she opened the rickety door, she saw the woodcutter had slaughtered the wolf and Grandma was extricated.

Najma Mohamed (12)

Trinity Academy, Leeds

WHEN DAY BREAKS

There was nothing more beautiful than a warm sunny morning, but this glorious setting very quickly turned to hell. People melted where they stood, a sudden, slow and painful death. Millions died globally. A short chorus of screams, then nothing.

The sun! It had finally turned on the Earth. An apocalypse of rotation. The other side had 12 hours before apocalypse... *tick, tick.*

Meanwhile, on the day side...

Screaming masses of pain and suffering roamed, searching the shadows, determined to drag them into the light to absorb them into their towering forms.

It was the end of the world.

Alex Robertson (15)
Turning Point Academy, Ormskirk

APOCALYPTIC

The world had changed. Fear, chaos and anarchy replaced the familiar. A new order formed. Nothing untouched. The dead: The undead.

Scanning to escape, eyes almond, narrowing and droopy; her frame skyscraping, waiting in the shadows. Blood ran from her cut eye, the last punishment for trying to escape. Outside a pitch-black city with inky skies, tremors and reverberations.

The stench of knife-edged razor blood filled the city. Loaded and leaden the smack of smoke from raging fires that devour. Bolting from the prison, hunting for the blood of zombies, the ones that created this world...

Keiran Mullock (15)
Turning Point Academy, Ormskirk

WHAT IF THE MINOTAUR KILLED THESEUS?

Theseus' mind was boggled beyond belief. All the twists and turns had shattered his morale. The string was useless in guiding him now through the seemingly endless maze. There was a loud snort and heavy thuds as the Minotaur inched closer. Poor Theseus had no idea what was about to happen to him as the dreadful beast turned the corner and its bloodthirsty eyes penetrated his soul. Giving Theseus no time to breathe, it charged into him, slamming its hefty horns deep into his chest. A quick squeal was all Theseus could muster before the labyrinth fell silent once again...

Louie Burman (13)
Tuxford Academy, Tuxford

THE DRAGON'S PERSPECTIVE...

I, quite simply, do not understand why it is that humans always feel the need to enter my cave and try slaying me. It is ever so boring and repetitive. What a coincidence that it always seems to happen while I'm trying to get some beauty sleep. The malicious men of the lands I end up going to always try to steal my hard-earned treasure by ending my already very dull and tedious life. They could always just ask, what happened to basic manners? Then I give them a small burn and they start acting like I killed their cat.

Auguste Birbalaite (14)
Tuxford Academy, Tuxford

URSULA

I swished angrily about in my cave, slapping my tentacles across endless rows of freshly plucked eyeballs. Snapping my fingers, the silver crystal ball closed, cutting the vision of Ariel brushing her red mane of hair and smiling that annoying smile of hers.

I caught a glimpse of myself in the cracked mirror. My face was contorted in rage as if I was sucking on a particularly sour lemon. Ariel danced around elegantly in my mind's eye, laughing at my horrid appearance.

Desperately smoothing down my awfully spiky hair, I glanced in the mirror again. The same monster stared back.

Maryam Mirza (12)
Twickenham School, Whitton

CROWNING COLOURS

Red and white. Night and day. Moon and sun. The two queens stood bickering in the hallway, creating an audience. "Well, I'm the eldest, you half-brain fool!" cried Iracebeth. "At least I haven't got that pompous head of yours - bet it doesn't even fit the tiara!" Mirana, the white queen, snickered, the crowd around her bursting into laughter. The red queen, Iracebeth, and Mirana weren't the most loving sisters; every day they bickered like this, and the school took Mirana's side. Prom queen gave someone the highest authority imaginable. If only they could see the darkness that lay within her.

Charlotte Porter (13)
Ursuline High School, Wimbledon

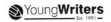

THE UNNOTICED EXISTENCE

Horns blared. Cruise ships raised their flags as they set sail through industries to the sea of freedom. Banners rose from crowds; ensembles performed stentorian fanfares. Blazing fireworks burnt across the sky; applauding cheers reverberated through the horizon.

Deep down in the waters, a dreary pair of impenetrable black eyes attracted, observing the smoke invading as its body merged inside the black. Drifting away, it retreated and lingered on the spot. Staring at the abandoned home, hollowness stretched along its heart. With some final waves of memories flooding back, the shark wriggled its eight fins and faded into the blue.

Gaia Lai (12)
Ursuline High School, Wimbledon

THE PURGE

26/07/74, 9:21
"All crimes are legal for 24 hours. Emergency services will not be in use."
Some kind of 'population control' the government thinks is a good idea. That is if you're excited about getting killed. If you aren't and your best friend is standing over your cowering body with a gun pointed at you, it's a bad idea.
"Being your friend is definitely the worst thing I've ever done. To see you like this, however, almost makes up for it."
Bang!
Hang on. I'm still alive?
"Come on, get up. I shot the camera. No one's watching us anymore."

Ines Cruz (12)
Ursuline High School, Wimbledon

DRIZELLA'S HAPPY ENDING

"The slipper fits!"

I glanced at Cinderella - poor girl didn't even get a chance to try the slipper on; how tragic! But that doesn't matter to me, this meant that my life would be more glamorous than it already was - the riches, the pearls and the prince were mine! Cinderella's sorrowful eyes watched as I entered the carriage. "Chin up, Cindy, you'll have less shoes to polish!" I jeered as the wheels bustled beneath me and took me away to my new life.

In the end, it's not always the one with the saddest story who gets their happy ending...

Sophia Brique (13)

Ursuline High School, Wimbledon

NIGHT AND DAY

Our lives were intertwined at dawn and dusk for that is where the blazing flames of her unrequited love first arose in my blind-sided heart. She belonged to land held high in the sky; I was lost to the fortress of stars.

Her ethereal presence, the beating radiation of her downcast heart; my own thundering soul longed to ignite at the hand of her flame. My crestfallen eyes caught onto her flickering hues; I was drowning in emophilia.

And as the sun trawled beneath the horizon, my heart shattered at the thought of her light fading into the stygian void.

Eva Fletcher (13)
Ursuline High School, Wimbledon

DOOM?

My palms were sweating profusely as we were all taken away from the grand hall. The place which seemed so inviting, now made me sick.

"You'll be taken to the labyrinth at dawn," a voice barked.

I was shaking. This was the end. We were forced into a small cell for the night, the lights were out. Leaving us in the dark. Soon, the whispers arose. Then - silence. I drifted off to sleep, only to be woken up by... "Okay, I'll meet you in the morning with the items," breathed a voice before scuttling away. What was going on?

Hiba Usama (13)
Ursuline High School, Wimbledon

A PUMPKIN'S NEGLECT

I sat alone in the dirt, rotting away as neglect had taken its toll on me. Abruptly, I felt like my legs were being pulled off as I got disconnected from my lonely life in the soil but this wasn't worth it as all I felt was agony and the breeze trying to soothe me with its cool pinch. *Plunk!* I was dropped onto the cold, hard floor.

A burning sensation came over me. It felt like my insides were being turned inside out, but then it stopped and I felt myself transform...

Keira Nair (13)

Ursuline High School, Wimbledon

TASK FORCE

The Task Force runs, there are too many tangos now. "They're everywhere," Price says, breathing heavily, all of them weak. "Shepherd, rest for now."
They run and run and run. Then all of a sudden, Soap gets shot. "Argh!" he exclaims.
"Soap, it'll be alright!" Price says stretching his arm, picking up Soap. "There! It's Shepherd in that car!" They all run towards it and jump in.
"P-Price... you need to know..." He gets cut off when Shepherd unexpectedly jumps out of the car. Then *bang!* They wake up to see Shepherd with a gun at Soap's head. Shepherd shoots...

George Mills (13)
Waterhead Academy, Oldham

THE HOT SAVANNAH

Any second now she should be home. How late can Abeba be? I'm going to look outside. Should I be worried?

Keeping an eye out for a young girl, I finally noticed my daughter lying shrivelled on the floor. The savannah sure is hot! I was going to use her father but she'll be just fine. Cradling her through the door, I placed her limp body down, tearing her limb by limb until she finally fitted in the oven. Mark (her father) entered at the right time for tea. "Where's Abeba?" he questioned.

"Oh don't worry dear, she's right here..."

Lola Williams (12)
Waterhead Academy, Oldham

BOB

Once upon a time, there was this boy called Bob and he was nine years old. His family was really poor.

One day, an army came to attack Bob and his family so they got scared and began to hide but the attackers found Bob so his mother said to him, "I'm sorry," and took the bullet for Bob. Then, *boom!* Bob's entire family was dead and Bob got so mad and unintentionally blasted the whole army away. Then he realised he had powers so he bravely and angrily got up and attacked and won!

Anees Hussain (13)
Waterhead Academy, Oldham

THE RISE OF THE DEAD

Sat in the corner of my room sobbing after my grandad told me my grandma had died, submerging my thoughts on a piece of paper. My grandad had told me about a potion that brings dead people back to life but you need an elephant's trunk. Spending day after day feeding it plants we became best friends until one day I tore its trunk off. I went home with it and to my surprise, my grandma's chair had her in it. My grandad was a liar! I killed an elephant! I committed a crime!

Alfie Riley (12)

Waterhead Academy, Oldham

WHAT IF ANAKIN WASN'T FOLLOWED BY OBI-WAN...

Anakin had just arrived on Mustafar and looked around to see if anyone had followed him. Out of the corner of his eye, he saw a familiar ship coming in for landing. A familiar little green man walked out of the ship and said, "Come to Coruscant, you must."

Anakin replied, "Make me!" and tried to strike Yoda down, but Yoda dodged and struck him with his tiny green lightsaber and Anakin gave in. The pair climbed onto the ship and travelled back to Coruscant, where the Jedi Order discussed Anakin's punishment for murdering all of the younglings...

Alfie Ryan (12)
Wellfield Community School, Wingate

THE GREED OF THE PEOPLE

Long ago, the city of Athens had entered a dark side. The citizens of the city were using the city's wealth for their greed. The gods were disappointed by the city. Zeus became angrier every day at what the city was doing. His wife tried to calm him down, but Zeus had had enough. He sent out the wildest lightning storm. The city of Athens crumbled as lightning and rain fell all around the city. The people of Athens realised their mistake. This lightning storm was sent because of their greed. The citizens of Athens never committed greed again.

Aioan Hall (12)
Wellfield Community School, Wingate

ROMEO AND JULIET

Romeo couldn't believe his eyes. He walked in on Juliet. She lay still. A shiver shot down Romeo's spine. He rushed over to her. Another shiver shot down his back as he saw her lying stiller than a statue. He placed the back of his hand on her forehead. Romeo didn't know what to do. His wife, dead. Without thinking he drove his dagger into himself. Juliet was waking up from her sleeping potion. She looked down but all she saw was a dark rippling pool underneath Romeo. She was distraught.

Three years later, Juliet is living and happily married.

Ellis Yates (13)
West Derby School, West Derby

234

THE BETRAYAL

I betrayed Hansel, my brother. We'd been kidnapped by the witch and there was no other choice. But there was a choice. A choice I didn't take. My brother is dead. I guess it's my fault. The witch made me a wicked offer; sacrifice my brother and I would be free to go. But I didn't go. Not because the witch lied or because I was trapped in any way. I chose to stay. I chose to watch him burn in the oven and his horrific screams still pierce my ears. Oh, I must say, roasted human tastes quite nice.

Esha Ajith (14)
Westfield Academy, Yeovil

BRAVE BLACK RIDING HOOD

I stand, my heart thumping, at the edge of the door. My camouflaged coat, once red, wrapped around me. This wolf killed my family. Now, my mission is to kill him. My radar starts to beep, sensing movement from inside. I turn it off and ready the laser gun poised in my hand. This is my moment. My hands shake, but I steel myself; now is no time for weakness. It goes by so fast, a sudden movement, a flash of laser fire, a billow of wretched fur, and I have done it. For I am Brave Black Riding Hood.

Kiara Huntly (12)
Winterbourne Academy, Winterbourne

ALIEN ENCOUNTER

School, a horrifying place to be, well it's called 'skool' for some reason. It was hard to fall asleep after the experience I experienced last night. The teacher had called, a new student had joined us. Something didn't feel right, the kid had green skin, no ears, no nose, and three fingers covered with black gloves. I pointed hesitantly at the so-called 'kid'. This must be the alien I'd heard through a transmission last night, he was here to conquer the planet. Well, that's what I heard from that transmission. I had to stop his villainous deeds... no matter what...

Bethany Burns
Workington Academy, Workington

YoungWriters®
Est. 1991

YOUNG WRITERS
INFORMATION

We hope you have enjoyed reading this book – and that you will continue to in the coming years.

If you're a young writer who enjoys reading and creative writing, or the parent of an enthusiastic poet or story writer, do visit our website **www.youngwriters.co.uk**. Here you will find free competitions, workshops and games, as well as recommended reads, a poetry glossary and our blog. There's lots to keep budding writers motivated to write!

If you would like to order further copies of this book, or any of our other titles, then please give us a call or order via your online account.

Young Writers
Remus House
Coltsfoot Drive
Peterborough
PE2 9BF
(01733) 890066
info@youngwriters.co.uk

Join in the conversation!
Tips, news, giveaways and much more!

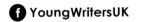 YoungWritersUK  YoungWritersCW 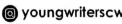 youngwriterscw